Podcasts, Pretenders & Pumpkins

A Willowcroft Cozy Mystery Book Three

Fran Heap

This is a work of fiction. The characters, locations, businesses, events and incidences are products of the author's imagination. Any resemblance to actual persons living or dead, or actual events is purely coincidental.

First published by Frances Heap contactable at fran@franheapwriter.com

A catalogue record for this book is available from the National Library of Australia

Cover design by 100Covers.

Created with Atticus

Willowcroft Map

View larger color version on website via QR code.

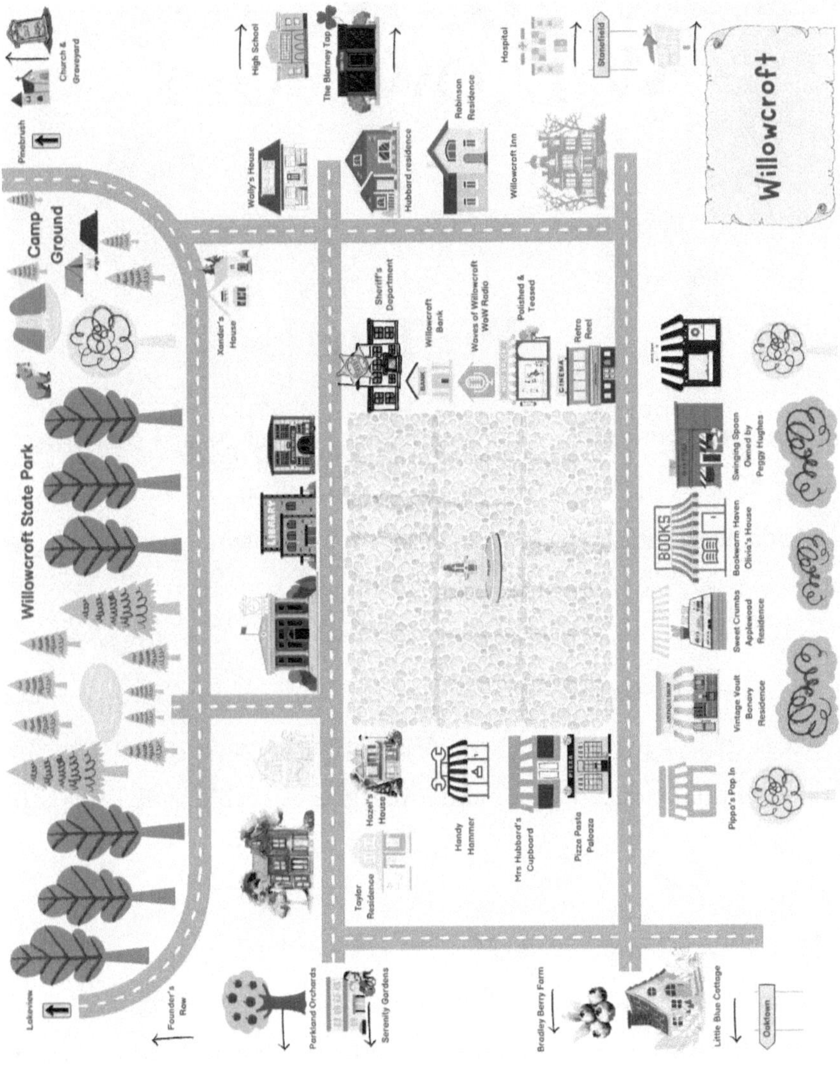

www.franheapwriter.com/willowcroft-map/

WELCOME TO WILLOWCROFT

A quick refresher for returning sleuths and a handy guide for newcomers.

The Team

Tammy Rumbelow – Thriller/mystery writer turned cozy mystery writer. New to Willowcroft from Los Angeles since the summer. Lives in the little blue cottage just outside of town. Her last thriller review stated: "She's not just over 40, she's over, full stop."

Olivia Huddlestone – Owner of Bookworm Haven bookstore with a genealogy side gig. Moved from Manhattan 15 years ago after turning twenty-one. Curious to a fault and loves food but can't cook. Lives above her store.

Mrs. Hazel Temperance (Mrs. T) – Retired history teacher, knitting circle matriarch, and widow of the town's late doctor, Harold. Daughter of a British WW2 war bride, Elsie. Born in Willowcroft. Known for her colorful shawls and occasional Britishisms. Lives in the northwest corner of the square in the old doctor's surgery and residence.

Wally – Retired town sheriff with a Boston Homicide background. Divorced with children and grandchildren all living in Boston. Lives three doors down from the north-east corner of the square and the Sheriff's Department.

Xander Simmons – Tech-savvy teen who'd rather code than socialize. Won a teenage comedy night competition at the local radio station. His dad is Park Ranger Dan, who oversees the state park bordering town.

Lockie (Pawlock Holmes) – Tammy's adopted stray cat. An integral member of the team who sniffs out clues that humans miss. A town celebrity after helping apprehend the instigator in the Willowcroft Great Bear Caper.

The Willow-Crafters (Knitting Circle & *Knotty but Nice* group text)

Betty – Romance obsessed. Hazel's best friend since childhood.

Marjorie Hubbard – Stern, prim, and proper. Keeper of the grapevine, though she'd never admit it. Married to Gerald.

Della Mae Beasley – Bit of a hoarder. Married to Roger.

Beatrice Smith – Can't do a slip stitch to save herself.

Other Townsfolk

Nick Bradley – Classmate of Xander's doing Community Service for his summer pranks.

Maxine – Town librarian.

Bev – Administrator for the Sheriff's Department and keeper of the department's archives key. Promised Wally he could access the archives whenever he needed after he solved a cold case that brought closure to a former resident's murder.

Eleanor Bennett (formerly Cross) – Lives in Serenity Gardens care facility, friends with Hazel and Marjorie.

Max Cross – Eleanor's older brother. In a state of advanced dementia prior to his death last summer at Serenity Gardens.

Nathan Cross – Max's grandson, currently residing in a forensic psychiatric hospital.

Mrs. Robinson – Sister-in-law to a skeleton, Cathy, found in the tunnels.

Willowcroft's Town Square Businesses

Bookworm Haven – Olivia's cozy bookstore. Headquarters for sleuthing, featuring a hidden bookcase door and a murder board. Olivia lives in the apartment above. (Nestled between the bakery and diner.)

Sweet Crumbs – The town bakery owned by Mr. and Mrs. Applewood. She is the town hugger and famous for her apple pie, which no one else in town sells.

The Swinging Spoon – A classic diner owned by Peggy Hughes, known for its pancakes and cherry pie.

Mrs. Hubbard's Cupboard – Local grocery store run by the current Mrs. Hubbard, Katie. It was previously run by Marjorie Hubbard, Katie's mother-in-law, and by Marjorie's mother-in-law before that. It's known for providing the best and most up-to-date gossip in town.

Waves of Willowcroft (WoW) – Local radio station. Held a teen comedy competition in the summer, which Xander won. Housed in the basement that once formed part of the Willowcroft Bank.

Willowcroft Bank – Scene of a 1954 bank heist, which has only recently been solved and the money recovered. The building has been subdivided over the years.

The Retro Reel – Willowcroft's old-school movie theater.

Pizza Pasta Pallooza – Local pizza delivery service offering other meals as well.

Vintage Vault – Antique store owned by Mr. Bonavy.

Polished and Teased – Local hair and nail salon run by Vanessa and Bree.

Pippa's Pop Ins – Short-term rental for businesses.

Handy Hammer – Hardware Store.

Off the Town Square

Serenity Gardens – Nursing home/care facility overlooking Parkland Orchards. Nurse Emma is a regular staff member known for her wacky medical scrub designs.

Willowcroft Inn – Only inn in town, run by George and Georgina Gregson.

Willowcroft State Park Campground – Located on the east side of the park, known for its bear sightings. It has a bear cam app.

The Blarney Tap – An Irish pub.

Parkland Orchards – An apple farm where Mrs. Applewood (formerly Parkland) grew up.

Bradley Berry Farm – Known for its blueberries and blueberry honey.

Drive-In – Opened in 1954, located on the road out of town toward the highway and Stonefield.

Towns of Greater Willowcroft

Stonefield – Shopping Plaza, Hospital, Library (its own)

Oaktown – Cozy Corner Cafe

Lakeview – Mrs. Bennett's home from when she married until entering Serenity Gardens.

Pinebrush

Chapter 1

Rowe Harvey's rental car scattered crimson and gold leaves as she swerved to a halt outside Willowcroft's Town Hall. The Michigan fall swirled around her like the unanswered questions that had drawn her here.

Stepping out, she buttoned her trench coat against the sharp wind. The carefully curated charm of the square triggered immediate distrust. Too perfect. Too rehearsed. Her journalist's instincts were sounding alarms.

"Spooktacular Halloween Festival" banners snapped between lamp-posts topped with plastic skulls grinning down at unsuspecting tourists. Orange and purple bunting festooned the quaint storefronts. The aroma of caramel apples and pumpkin spice hung in the air like an olfactory cliché. Rowe allowed herself a cynical smile. Places this determined to appear idyllic always had the darkest secrets.

"Ms. Harvey!" A man with a notepad and a tie patterned with tiny black bats bustled toward her, hand outstretched, enthusiasm radiating from him like heat. "Thomas Berry, Willowcroft Gazette. We're absolutely thrilled you've chosen our humble town for your podcast."

"Cut the pleasantries." She adjusted the recorder in her hand, thumb hovering over the record button. "Where's the action?"

He shrugged and gestured toward the cluster of awnings nestled beneath flame-colored maples. "Right this way." He took off with a skip. "Olivia's bookstore is where I suggest you start."

Rowe scanned from Sweet Crumbs bakery's towering pies to Bookworm Haven's quaint displays and the Swinging Spoon diner's flashing neon. Every inch screamed postcard polish. But two murders and a bank heist told a different story. Beyond the bunting and baked goods lurked rot she intended to expose. The evidence had led her here months ago.

Her true crime podcast about the Prohibition-era tunnels and the seventy-year-old money trail would captivate her listeners, but Rowe pursued another goal. Something personal she kept to herself.

Her feet pounded the cobblestoned square. Thomas huffed behind her.

"How's your research coming along?" he asked when he caught up outside the bookstore.

"No shortage of actual news elsewhere." She eyed the garish purple of Mrs. Hubbard's Cupboard grocery store across the street. "I didn't abandon an election scandal for recipes and photo contests."

Fallen leaves spiraled around Rowe's boots. She gripped her lapels and squared her shoulders. Thomas's eager grin faltered.

"I'm here for the real story." Her fingers drummed against her device. "The truth behind this town's skeletons. Not the glossy brochure version."

She pushed through the bookstore's door without waiting for his response.

A woman with glasses and a cardigan peered up from her spot at the counter. "Hello! Welcome to the Bookworm Haven. Are you here for the preview?"

Rowe pressed record and thrust her microphone at the woman. "Rowe Harvey. True crime podcaster. You must be Olivia."

The woman's eyes widened. "Yes, that's me. I'm—"

"The owner of this bookstore and ticket vendor for the Willowcroft Tunnel Museum." She bent forward. "Tell me about those tunnels. How did they stay hidden for so long?"

Olivia blinked twice. "They were well-concealed. We only discovered them—"

"Because you were searching for the bank heist money." Rowe studied the tiny flinch in Olivia's expression. "Walk me through what happened."

Olivia's fingers straightened a stack of bookmarks on the counter. "It's quite a story. It began this past summer when Tammy moved to town and found a threatening letter in her attic."

"In the little blue cottage where the cash was stashed?"

"Yes." Olivia's eyebrow rose. "Tammy was a new resident, but we'd already met when she stopped by my store. She brought me the letter not long after, and that's when things started to snowball. Our little group came together soon after."

"How so?"

"We'd all been caught up in the Great Willowcroft Bear Caper. Wally, Mrs. T—sorry, Mrs. Temperance—and I each had bear visits, and we worked with Xander and Lockie the cat to catch the teenager who was luring the bears into town."

Olivia gave a soft chuckle. "That's when we realized we enjoyed solving mysteries."

"And once Ms. Rumbelow arrived?"

"We connected the letter to Mary Collins's murder. A seventy-year-old locked-room case. Totally unsolved."

A family entered the store. Rowe's foot tapped against the wooden floor as Olivia excused herself. *Convenient interruption.* She eyed the flyers by the register advertising the museum courtesy bus while Olivia explained the schedule to the customers.

When the family left with their purchases, Rowe pounced. "The murder led you to the bank heist?"

"In a roundabout way." Olivia's shoulders relaxed. "While investigating Mary's death, we found she was linked to a cold case robbery that took place three weeks earlier. No one had considered them connected until then."

"And your team?" Rowe prompted. "What qualifies a bookseller, a..." She pretended to consult her notes, though she had memorized the details. "...a retired detective, a tech specialist, and a town gossip to crack a case the authorities couldn't solve in seventy years?"

Olivia ground her teeth. "Mrs. Temperance is not a gossip. She's a local matriarch with invaluable knowledge about Willowcroft."

She inhaled deeply. "And we each brought something unique: Wally's investigative experience, Xander's technical skills, my research abilities specializing in genealogy, Tammy's writer perspective, and Lockie was instrumental."

"A cat," Rowe said. *Is this woman serious?* "So you solved the murder, then went hunting for the loot?"

"Once we identified Max Cross as Mary's killer, yes." Olivia's eyes brightened. "That search led us to discover the tunnels built during Prohibition, and to Cathy Robinson's skeleton."

"Mary's lover and accomplice in the heist."

"Yes." Olivia's voice softened. "They stumbled upon the vault entrance and stole the cash, but they didn't get the happy ending they'd hoped for."

"And how did you find it? After seventy years, it seems remarkably convenient."

Olivia hesitated before answering. "Max Cross's grandson, Nathan, had notes from his grandfather's dementia ramblings. They brought us back to Tammy's place, where the money had been hidden under the attic floorboards all along."

"And where Mary was murdered," Rowe said. "Poetic justice."

"I suppose you could say that."

"And now you've turned tragedy into tourism." Rowe jerked her chin toward the museum flyers. "Tell me how this operation works."

Olivia's shoulders dropped. "We provide a shuttle service." She pointed out the window as a vintage-styled vehicle parked by the curb. "It takes visitors from here to the tunnel entrance by Tammy's cottage. The tour goes through the safe portions of the tunnels and ends at the Swinging Spoon diner back in town."

"Efficient." Rowe eyed the bus. "And who does what in this enterprise?"

"Tammy, Wally, and Xander lead the tours. Each shares their own perspective based on how they helped solve the case. Mrs. Temperance runs the exhibition room, where we've displayed artifacts and a story timeline."

"And your role?"

"I sell the tickets here and maintain the historical documentation." Olivia gestured to a display of books about Prohibition and local lore arranged near the counter.

"I'll be speaking with all of them." She slipped the recorder into her pocket and angled toward the door. "Your small-town charm has been… illuminating."

"I hope you have a wonderful stay," Olivia called after her as Rowe headed for the exit.

Outside, her fingers curled into fists. The operation was slick, she'd give them that. A blend of history and entertainment. But Willowcroft won't know what hit it after she was finished.

I'm the trick to this town's Halloween treat.

Chapter 2

Olivia stepped back from the window display, palms dusted with gold powder and fingertips sticky with glue. A miniature pumpkin sat nestled at the base of the art deco lamp. Playful shadows danced across the silk fringe as glass beads cascaded around a flapper's beaded dress. Perfect. She'd spent three hours arranging each element until the 1920s scene practically vibrated with jazz, illicit whiskey, and a hint of Halloween mischief.

The bell above the door jingled. Mr. Bonavy from the Vintage Vault antique store a few doors down materialized in the doorway like a ghost conjured by the season, shoulders hunched, face drawn into unfamiliar lines. He worked the felt hat in his hands, twisting the brim into soft accordion pleats.

"Mr. Bonavy?" The satisfaction drained from Olivia's chest. "You're back already?"

He stared past her, zeroing in on the antique register, which gleamed beneath the spiderweb bunting she'd draped across the front counter.

His lips pressed into a bloodless line. "That's the one," he said, stepping inside. "The brass cash register."

"You recognize your own merchandise?" Olivia teased to lighten the mood.

He gave a half-hearted chuckle. "Can I check something?"

Olivia blinked. "Is something wrong with it?"

"No... I don't know." He walked closer. "A Ms. Harvey came to see me. Asked about it. Wanted to know where it came from. If I'd checked for hidden compartments."

"Hidden compartments?" Olivia echoed, her curiosity igniting like a candle in a jack-o'-lantern. She followed his gaze to the register. "It's from the 1920s, you said?"

"Roughly. It's the kind they used in old general stores. No brand name, just those solid brass keys and the original drawer." He rubbed his palms on his jacket. "But now I keep wondering... What if she knew something? What if there's something inside it? A document or some tucked-away item that could be... misunderstood."

"You have done nothing wrong."

"I haven't," he agreed quickly. "But she has a way of making you believe like you have."

Olivia stepped around the counter, eyes gleaming with restrained excitement. "Well, now we have to check."

Mr. Bonavy hesitated. "You don't mind?"

"Are you kidding?" She ran her fingers along the ridged brass keys. "This is history and mystery in one polished package." *This is delicious.*

He cracked a smile. "Don't say that. You'll make my price go up."

She slipped her hands behind the register, tracing its ornate curves. "Let's start methodically. Top to bottom, inside to out."

Mr. Bonavy's hands hovered, stalled by some antique version of stage fright. He touched the "No Sale" key like it might bite and pressed it. The drawer shot out with a satisfying cha-ching.

"The obvious place would be in here." Olivia lifted the metal cash tray, peering underneath. "Nothing but dust and... wait." She extracted a yellowed receipt and examined it. "A bill for cigars."

She dropped to her knees, squinting at the underside of the machine. "Secret spaces were common during Prohibition. People concealed all sorts of things."

Mr. Bonavy tapped the brass sides. "Listen for hollow spots."

"Good idea." Olivia rapped her knuckles along the casing, angling her head to detect any difference. "Solid here... here too..." She paused. "This section sounds different."

He produced a small screwdriver from his pocket. "Antique dealer's best friend."

"You came prepared."

"When Ms. Harvey mentioned hidden sections, I got curious."

He loosened four tiny screws from the baseplate. The metal panel came away, revealing nothing but ancient gears.

Disappointing. "Let's check the display window."

"The keys themselves might be important." Mr. Bonavy examined each one. "Sometimes they form a code."

She pressed a series of numbers in combination to make cards pop up behind the glass, something she'd read in a novel. Nothing unexpected appeared. Deflating.

Olivia jiggled the drawer. "This spring is stiff."

"That's normal for this model."

"Is it?" She reached for a letter opener, sliding its thin edge behind the coin section. Her tongue poked between her teeth as she probed. "Something's catching here..."

A click echoed through the quiet store. They froze.

"Did you hear that?" Mr. Bonavy asked.

She carefully wiggled the tool deeper. Another click, followed by the soft metallic sound of a spring releasing.

"There's a mechanism here." *This is simply scrumptious.* She pressed at a different angle.

Nothing.

She tried again, holding her breath as the metal slipped further. It met resistance, then gave way with a satisfying snap. But instead of revealing a secret chamber, the old spring reset itself with a disappointing clang.

"False alarm." Olivia withdrew. "The original workings, nothing more."

"I suppose that's a relief."

"No trapdoors. No hidden compartment with a long-lost key."

Mr. Bonavy let out a breath, tension softening in his posture. "So it's… what it seems?"

"An old cash box with perfect patina," she said. "And exactly the right vibe for the museum's ticket desk."

He stepped back. "Well. Thank you for indulging my nerves."

She smiled. "If there'd been a secret, we'd have found it. I was rooting for one."

Mr. Bonavy adjusted his hat. "That woman got in my head. That's all. Glad to see it's merely a machine and not a ticking time bomb."

"Some days," Olivia said, patting the register fondly, "being just a machine is enough."

The antique dealer returned to his store with more relaxed shoulders than when he'd arrived.

Olivia's stomach growled. Playing treasure hunter had awakened her appetite. She glanced at the wall clock. Time for a quick bite before her afternoon regulars started wandering in.

She scrawled a note: Next door. And taped it to the counter beside a mini witch's cauldron filled with bookmarks.

Olivia entered Sweet Crumbs expecting comfort and cinnamon, but the usual baking-with-love bustle was missing. Mrs. Applewood stood at the prep station, arms folded, staring down at a sagging pie as if it had personally betrayed her.

Olivia approached. "Everything okay?"

The older woman didn't turn to her. "No. And yes. And no."

Olivia waited.

Mrs. Applewood sighed. "I've made six. Not one came out right. The crust won't flake. The filling's too thin. I even—" she lowered her voice like she was confessing a crime, "—I even forgot my secret ingredient in the first one."

Olivia gasped.

"My hands have forgotten how to bake."

"That's not possible," Olivia said. "Your apple pies have won first place nine years in a row."

"Ten," she said, then flinched. "That's what she said, too."

"Who?"

Mrs. Applewood looked up, her eyes cloudy. "That podcaster woman sat at the corner table with her little notebook. Said she was doing a feature on local traditions. Said my pies were legendary."

"That sounds nice."

"She didn't mean it as a compliment." Mrs. Applewood gripped the edge of the counter. "She smiled that awful little smile and asked who on the judging panel I'd been paying off. Said no one could be *that* consistent without help. Said it wasn't natural."

Olivia's stomach turned. "That's horrible."

"She said people talk. Claimed I wasn't as sweet as my apple glaze." Her voice cracked. "I haven't baked right since."

Behind them, the mixer gave a soft whirr. Mr. Applewood peeked out from the kitchen, holding a tray of unbaked cupcakes.

"She's lying, of course," he said. "About the judges. Everyone loves your pies. And no one has ever guessed the secret ingredient."

Mrs. Applewood shook her head. "I should've said something. Kicked her out."

The older woman wiped her hands on her apron. "She made me believe I'd cheated at something I've loved doing my whole life."

"Then make one more," Olivia said. "A redemption pie."

Mrs. Applewood gave a watery laugh. "I like that. Redemption pie. If it turns out, I'll know I'm still me."

Mr. Applewood beamed. "I'll peel the apples."

Chapter 3

The October chill seeped through the cracks of Hazel Temperance's Victorian home as darkness claimed Willowcroft. Orange and purple fairy lights twinkled from neighboring porches, while carved pumpkins grinned from stoops across the historic cobblestone square beyond the front door.

Hazel tugged her bright marigold shawl tighter. "Tea before bedtime keeps the monsters at bay," she murmured, channeling her mother's voice with a hint of a British lilt that appeared occasionally despite being Michigan-born and raised.

In the kitchen, she filled the copper kettle Harold had given her on their fifteenth wedding anniversary. The familiar weight anchored her to memories of his practical nature, his unwavering preference for beige sweaters, and silence over fuss.

The gift went onto the stove as she caught a reflection in the window. Silver hair, vibrant shawl, a glint of mischief. Harold would've hated the color. The thought produced a smile.

While the water heated, she plated the last blueberry scone. The recipe came straight from her mother Elsie, who had crossed the Atlantic as a war bride, bringing little more than a recipe box and stories of a bombed-out London. The scent of vanilla and berries filled the kitchen, transporting Hazel back to childhood Sunday afternoons.

"Proper scones need proper jam," she said to the empty room. "Though Mom would faint dead away at this honey nonsense."

The kettle whistled. Hazel warmed the teapot first, as mother had insisted, before measuring loose Earl Grey leaves and pouring the boiling water. Steam curled upward, perfuming the air with bergamot.

With the tray prepared, she carried it to the cozy, cluttered living room. Fabrics of every shade draped the furniture: scarlet throws, emerald pillows, indigo afghans. Hand-knit shawls hung from hooks like prized plumes, each one a rebellion against Harold's fondness for neutral tones.

She settled into the reading chair positioned to view both the fireplace and the cobblestone square through the bay window. Jack-o'-lanterns flickered outside, casting dancing shadows across the historic stones she and others had fought so hard to preserve decades ago. Marjorie, ever the gossip hound, had sworn she'd discovered something buried in the council minutes before they voted to keep them. But she'd been maddeningly quiet about it since.

"What would the square be without its history?" Hazel broke off a scone corner and dabbed it with cream and a drizzle of the last of the Bradley Berry Farm blueberry honey. "Nothing but tarmac and regret."

The carriage clock ticked on the mantel. Beside it sat a silver-framed photograph of Harold, eternally stern in his doctor's coat.

"You'd have a conniption if you saw me now." She lifted her mug in mock salute. "Not a beige stitch in sight."

Five years gone, and still she conversed with him daily.

"You'd have hated this one," she added as she opened her latest book. "Too many dramatic flourishes. But the constable reminds me of you. Sensible to a fault."

She glanced at the photo of Elsie standing proud in a wartime ATS uniform. Hazel wished her mother had shared more about those years, but the woman always joked about signing the Official Secrets Act and being unable to breathe a word without facing trial for treason.

I suspect she liked the drama.

Her lips quirked again as her attention drifted to the sideboard, where a folder marked *Tunnel Museum* lay beneath a stack of craft magazines.

Life had taken a turn since Tammy Rumbelow arrived in town with a heart full of questions. In just a few months, Hazel had gone from a quiet retirement filled with scones and knitting to chasing cold cases with a ragtag crew including Tammy, Olivia, Wally, young Xander, and of course, Lockie the cat, who thought nothing of curling into a ball on top of important documents mid-investigation.

Their new venture would open soon, and Hazel knew much of her time would be swept up in manning the ticket desk with the Willow-Crafters knitting circle ladies. But she wouldn't have it any other way.

An owl hooted. The maple brushed its limbs against the windowpane. No mysterious thumps, or bears scratching at the door, or tickets to collect tonight. Nothing but tea and novels before her life changed again.

Whiskey burned down Wally's throat. The drink had a whole new meaning after being knee-deep in Prohibition history the past few months.

Outside, an ancient oak creaked. Two years or even a few months ago, that sound would have triggered his detective instincts. Now it belonged to the rhythm of retirement.

Twenty-four months since he'd pinned his sheriff's badge to the shadowbox. The past months had jolted him out of his quiet existence. First the bear incident, then Tammy arrived, and now he was part of a team investigating cold cases.

"Beats sitting around waiting to die."

His phone pinged. Xander texted about the upcoming tunnel tours. The kid's passion for their makeshift investigation team surpassed anything from Wally's twenty years with the Boston PD.

Last week, the boy installed a program on his phone. Should that bother him? Probably. Did it? No. The kid's tech skills had already unlocked crucial leads.

Wally jabbed a reply with his index finger, ignoring Xander's thumb-typing lessons.

Photos lined the walls. Children. Grandchildren. Milestones he'd missed during his years in Homicide. The Commissioner's commendation collected dust in the corner, hidden behind Liam's crayon masterpiece from last Christmas.

His glass sat empty. With a grunt and cracking knees, he levered himself out of the recliner. He studied the street from the window. Marjorie Hubbard's home blazed with Halloween decorations. Plastic skeletons climbed her porch columns. Mechanical witches cackled in the front yard.

Prim, proper Marjorie, who complained about wind chimes, transformed into Halloween's biggest champion every October. The woman contained multitudes.

The phone vibrated again. Another text from Xander.

His evening routine had changed for sure. Whiskey and books remained, but history ruled his nights now. The emptiness of retirement he'd feared had surrendered to purpose.

Olivia staggered up the narrow staircase, three bulging research binders threatening to slip from her grasp. She nudged past the even smaller kitchenette than the one downstairs and deposited the heavy load beside the sofa built for one with a thud.

After fifteen years in Willowcroft, her evenings were transforming. Where Agatha Christie novels once reigned supreme, maps and historical records now claimed their place. The bear incident and Tammy's arrival had upended that quiet existence for the better.

She flicked on the electric kettle. Some traditions, like nightly cocoa, remained non-negotiable.

Her fingers sifted through color-coded folders scattered across the floor. Bookstore ownership hadn't prepared Olivia for amateur detective work, but the meticulous organization of genealogy research projects transferred perfectly. Her mother back in Manhattan would have sneered at such fussy systems.

Her phone chimed. Tammy was texting about the museum. The thriller writer had blown into town mere months ago and had become the friend Olivia had always craved, someone who understood that "curiosity killed the cat," but that "information brought him back."

She swapped her everyday glasses for the bright pink frames perched on the side table. "Tragically librarian," Olivia's sister had called them once. They were a badge of honor now.

Steam billowed as hot water met cocoa powder and pumpkin spice in a novelty mug painted with tiny witches on broomsticks. The rich chocolate aroma filled the small apartment above the store while Willowcroft's secrets waited in the binders. Historical research had supplanted fiction in her new nighttime ritual.

Her fingers traced pencil lines connecting generations of local residents on the family trees she'd constructed. Dates and names created a spider's web of connections across the page.

The fountain lights in the town square blinked to life outside the window. Paper bats hung from the lampposts, and a lopsided wizard hat sat atop the war memorial. Children would soon be parading through with baskets swinging and costumes askew. How many of them had grandparents or great-grandparents connected to the mysteries they were unraveling?

Her phone chimed again with another message about the museum.

The bookstore owner who'd escaped Manhattan's suffocating social whirl now hunted small-town forgotten stories with the same intensity she once reserved for devouring Christie novels until dawn. Each discovery only spawned more questions, and every clue was a flavor she couldn't get enough of.

The memory of her twenty-first birthday lingered, fresh as if it were yesterday. That was the day Olivia's father skipped the lavish party of her sister's coming of age and bought the store instead. One night of Manhattan revelry versus a lifetime in Michigan. She had made the better deal. Her curiosity could never have been satisfied in a world of shallow cocktail conversations when there were so many mysteries waiting to be solved.

Chapter 4

Tammy's back screamed in protest. She hauled the last massive pumpkin into position along the path, grimacing as her muscles strained. It must have weighed thirty pounds. Worth it for the Halloween eve Jack-o'-Lantern Walk, though.

"This one's half-lead," she said, straightening and surveying the field.

The empty patch of land by her cottage had transformed into the entrance to Willowcroft's newest attraction. Caldwell's ancient Buick, a rusted monstrosity with mismatched doors, sat at the center. Its trunk was popped open to serve as an impromptu ticket booth. It creaked as if it might collapse at any moment.

"Swear that thing's haunted," Nick Bradley said, appearing beside her with a wooden sign tucked under his arm.

If only he knew how close to the truth he might be. The car had made clicking sounds all night. She'd never admit it to the others, but after everything they'd discovered in this town, she wouldn't rule out a car with paranormal leanings.

Nick's community service vest bore smears of dirt and orange paint. "Mrs. Temperance wants this out front." He displayed the hand-painted warning: WILLOWCROFT TUNNELS. ENTER AT OWN RISK!

Tammy wiped sweat from her forehead. "Put it by the hard hats."

Nick hammered the sign into place while Lockie stalked the perimeter of the museum entrance, tail twitching. He paused occasionally, ears perked toward the darkness, as if listening for something no one else could hear.

"That cat knows something we don't," Wally announced, trudging along the path with a stack of safety certificates in one hand and a collection of flashlights in the other. The ex-sheriff's weathered face creased into a smile. "Got our final approval this morning. These tunnels are officially not a death trap."

"High praise," Tammy said, accepting the paperwork. "Remind me to frame this. 'Not a death trap' should bring the tourists running."

Xander appeared from inside the museum, his laptop tucked under one arm. "Wi-Fi boosters are installed at all the junction points. The interactive map is working." He displayed a digital blueprint of the tunnel system on his screen. "Signal's strong all the way to the diner basement."

"The Willow-Crafters are ready for duty!" Mrs. Temperance, otherwise known as Mrs. T, called, marching across the field with the determination of a general and the knitwear of a champion. Her silver hair bobbed in a loose bun, and she clutched a bulging folder of notes like it was classified intel.

"They've been instructed to arrive at eight o'clock on the dot." She gave a crisp nod. "Each will wear their special knitted badge so visitors know who's in charge. And believe me, they like being in charge."

Leaning in as if sharing state secrets, she added, "The *Knotty but Nice* group chat is blowing up day and night. Betty's already crocheted a sash saying 'Tunnel Boss.'"

Tammy suppressed a grin. The idea of Willowcroft's senior knitting circle doubling as crowd control was both heartwarming and terrifying. Those ladies could knit a sweater and shame a teenager into obedience without dropping a stitch.

"Nick, directional arrows," Tammy pointed to a pile of wooden markers as if issuing a battlefield command. "Make sure they're bright enough to see in a blackout, or during a full-scale yarn rebellion."

He gave a mock salute. "Yes, ma'am. No one wants to get side-eyed by the scarf squad." He jogged off toward the paint with exaggerated urgency.

Wally snorted as he set the flashlights on the welcome table. "Speaking of impossible missions, I reinforced the junction where the water damage was. Again. It's now held together with more bolts than good sense."

"Olivia's finished the Mary and Cathy section," Mrs. T said. "She's captured their story beautifully." She handed Tammy a placard with an inscription.

Tammy ran her fingers over the words: Mary Collins and Catherine "Cathy" Robinson—separated by society, united in death.

"It's perfect," she said, a lump forming in her throat. "I'll place it in a prime position where everyone can appreciate the history."

"You know what this tunnel needs?" Marjorie Hubbard's voice boomed from behind them. She stood proudly in a Halloween sweater blinking with tiny light-up pumpkins, legs braced as if she were about to issue marching orders.

Marjorie's Halloween obsession strikes again.

Betty huffed beside her. "Please, not another one of your 'improveme nts.'"

"A ghost!" Marjorie declared, ignoring Betty. "A proper tunnel should have a ghost. I've brought my grandmother's wedding dress." She hoisted a plastic bag.

Betty rolled her eyes. "Last week it was motion-activated spiders, and before that—"

"The spiders were fantastic!" said Xander.

"They terrified the structural engineer," said Tammy. "The man nearly had a heart attack when one dropped on his head during the inspection."

Marjorie beamed. "Brilliant!"

"We are not hanging your grandmother's wedding dress from the ceiling," Betty said, leaving no room for argument.

Marjorie clutched the bag protectively. "Fine. I'll save it for the Christmas festival."

Marjorie turned to Tammy. "Did I tell you I'm bringing my famous pumpkin cookies tomorrow? Made with real pumpkin I grew myself."

"She means borrowed from Mrs. Hubbard's Cupboard," Betty stage-whispered.

"Betrayal!" Marjorie gasped. "I'll have you know those were for... decoration pumpkins!"

Tammy bit her lip to keep from laughing as the two women bickered all the way back across the field, their voices fading with distance while their arms waved with increasing enthusiasm.

Xander closed his laptop. "We should do one last walk-through. Check the safety rails and test the lighting."

"Lockie and I will head into town to confirm everything's set at Olivia's," Tammy said, "then meet you all at the diner to secure the exit point."

Mrs. T nodded. "The Willow-Crafters and I will finalize the welcome arrangements before joining you there."

Tammy hopped into her sedan and drove toward town, warmed by how everyone had come together to make this happen. Three months ago, they'd stumbled upon a hidden entrance in the field next to her cottage. Now, Willowcroft's underground history was about to be revealed to the world, or at least to the regional press and curious locals.

She slowed the car to take in the transformation. The once quaint, even sleepy square, now bustled with the energy she'd been trying to capture in her writing of late.

Fake spiderwebs draped store windows advertising "Tunnel Tour Specials," and skeletal figures lounged around the fountain like ghoulish guests at a party. Orange and black banners fluttered above the shops while workers hammered signs into place, directing visitors toward the museum. The Halloween touches stirred a lively hum of mischief and anticipation, making the whole town buzz. And she'd helped bring it to life.

Who could have imagined her spontaneous move from LA would lead to uncovering Willowcroft's hidden past?

Tammy parked outside Bookworm Haven, and the bell above the door announced her entrance.

"There's our museum owner and detective cat," Olivia called from behind a towering display of local history books. "How's the museum coming along?"

"If you can call a muddy field with a hole in it a museum, it's spectacular." Tammy navigated around precariously balanced book stacks. "Everything set for ticket sales tomorrow?"

Olivia walked to the counter and patted the antique cash register, her fingers lingering on the ornate edges with a wistfulness Tammy recognized. Olivia's treasure-hunt-thwarted face.

"Mr. Bonavy delivered this beauty," Olivia said, her voice dipping. "Said it dates back to the Prohibition era. He even thought there might be hidden compartments, but alas..." She sighed, shoulders dropping a fraction. "We didn't find any."

Tammy bit back a smile, recognizing the familiar blend of scholarly determination and childlike disappointment in her friend's tone. Olivia's endless quest for unearthing secrets was both endearing and contagious.

The brass machine gleamed under the store lights, its keys worn smooth from decades of use. She could practically see Olivia's imagination still running wild with visions of what might have been stashed inside during the town's bootlegging days.

Olivia adjusted a display of discounted tunnel-themed books. "Oh, I meant to tell you. Peggy mentioned hearing noises in the diner cellar again last night."

Tammy's interest piqued. "What noises?"

"Thumping. Scratching. The usual haunted basement repertoire." Olivia shrugged. "Probably the building settling, but with our history…"

"Or rats," Tammy added. "Speaking of the diner, I should head over. We're having a final meeting there."

"I'll close and join you."

They stepped from the bookstore to the Swinging Spoon next door. Its red neon lights blazed against the darkening sky, a beacon of 1950s nostalgia.

Peggy waved from behind the counter, her oversized cat-eye glasses adding to the vibe. "Museum crew in the corner booth!"

Tammy spotted Wally, Xander, and Mrs. T already squeezed into the large corner booth. Lockie claimed a spot on the vinyl seat.

"How'd the final inspection go?" Tammy slid in beside Wally.

Xander gave a thumbs-up. "The Wi-Fi mapping works perfectly. Tourists can track where they are in the tunnels on their phones."

"And the emergency signs are clear," Wally added. "Though we still need to work on wheelchair accessibility for the future."

"Speaking of," Mrs. T said, "did you work out how to get Mrs. Bennett down?"

Wally nodded. "I'll escort her through myself. At eighty-six, she deserves special accommodation. And it's her childhood dream to see them."

He paused, his eyes taking on the faraway glint he got when thinking of his family in Boston. "A few of us can help her down so she can fulfill her lifelong wish."

Tammy's chest gave a little squeeze, the good kind, like when a book ends just right. "That's wonderful. It'll mean the world to her."

Olivia nudged her glasses in that familiar signal Tammy now recognized as a transition to emotional topics. "I've heard from Mrs. Robinson. She's planning to attend the preview. It's bittersweet knowing her husband died without ever learning the truth about his sister, Cathy."

She sighed. "But Mrs. Robinson said it's comforting knowing Cathy's story will be remembered now. And her husband's spirit will be there too, smiling down on the exhibit in his big sister's honor."

Tammy reached over and squeezed Olivia's hand. "That's beautiful. I'm so glad we can bring closure to these families while sharing Willowcroft's past with everyone."

Peggy swooped in with a tray of milkshakes. "On the house, history-makers! And wait till you see tomorrow's special menu." She slapped down laminated cards featuring items like "Bootlegger's Burger" and "Smuggler's Fries."

"And my pièce de résistance," she added with a flourish, "Prohibition Punch!"

She pointed to a picture of a blood-red concoction, perfect for the season.

"Non-alcoholic, I hope," Mrs. T said.

Peggy winked. "For display purposes, sure."

Xander cleared his throat. "So, everything's set for tomorrow. Hard hats and flashlights are by the entrance, Willow-Crafters on crowd control, brochures at both ends."

"And a proper tribute to Mary and Cathy," Olivia said.

"To Mary and Cathy," they echoed, raising their milkshakes.

They exchanged jokes about the next day's schedule. Wally teased Xander about micromanaging the route, while Olivia bragged that her antique cash register would steal the show. Mrs. T detailed her plan to keep the lines orderly. Tammy soaked in every word, every smile. And, of course, the conversation turned to plans for the Jack-o'-Lantern Walk later.

Chapter 5

Hundreds of carved pumpkins bathed the town square in an eerie orange light, their ghoulish faces grinning from every windowsill, hay bale, and fence post. Goblins snarled, black cats arched their backs, and bats spread their wings, each one frozen in the fleeting immortality of gourd flesh.

Olivia yanked her scarf tighter against the October chill, her breath clouding as she squeezed through the mass of bodies gathered for the annual Jack-o'-Lantern Walk. The new route past the tunnel museum had turned the usual crowd into a crush of humanity.

"Coming through!" Wally bulldozed his way toward her, two steaming paper cups held high. "Spiced Vampire Punch, as requested. Extra cinnamon added because your lips are turning blue."

"You're a lifesaver." The heat burned through Olivia's mittens as she grabbed the cup. "Did the whole town come out tonight?"

"More like the entire county." Wally blew steam from his drink.

Children in costumes ricocheted between displays. A tiny devil shrieked with delight at a fanged pumpkin. Two miniature ghosts rushed past, white sheets billowing behind them, the scent of chocolate and candy apples trailing in their wake.

"Don't forget, you need all thirteen monster pumpkin tokens!" Mayor Marzolon's voice thundered across the square. "First child to bring me all tokens wins the honor of lighting the Great Glowing Gourd!"

The children scattered like startled crows. A little witch in a pointed hat seized her father's jacket sleeve, jabbing her finger toward a carved werewolf with pointy ears and a snarling mouth between two plain lanterns.

"That's one! Hurry, before someone else finds it!" Her tiny hand disappeared inside the hollowed gourd, emerging with a gleaming token.

The monster pumpkins lurked among hundreds of ordinary jack-o'-lanterns. Children zigzagged between displays like sugar-fueled phantoms, determined to collect all thirteen tokens before their competitors. Last year's winner had bragged until Valentine's Day.

Olivia sipped her punch, the cinnamon cranberry mix burning pleasantly down her throat. "The competition gets more intense every year. Those kids move faster than the Salem witch trials."

Wally snorted punch out of his nose. "Mayor Marzolon takes it way too seriously."

The Mayor preened on the town hall steps, his ceremonial sash reflecting the orange light. Elsbeth, the council secretary, hovered at his side, clipboard clutched to her chest like a shield against fun.

Wally jerked his chin toward Councilman Dean, who stood rigid at the edge of the walk, his mouth tight as he muttered to Sheriff Stanton. "Dean looks thrilled about the museum's popularity."

"Hardly his favorite project." The punch scalded Olivia's tongue.

The crowd surged forward as the procession began its journey from the Town Hall steps. Parents lit candles inside their children's pumpkins, the flames creating a shimmering trail of light that wound around the square.

Mrs. Temperance fluttered her fingers from across the street. The Willow-Crafters balanced carved gourds with intricate patterns. Beatrice Smith, who couldn't knit a slip stitch if her life depended on it, had transformed her pumpkin into an elaborate tableau of woodland creatures, guaranteeing her yet another win for best design.

"Olivia!" Tammy shoved through the crowd, Xander in her wake. "Have you seen Rowe Harvey lurking around town interviewing everyone?"

"She cornered me earlier." Xander rubbed his glasses with his shirttail.

"Great." A flicker of irritation sparked in Olivia's chest. That woman's microphone had appeared in every corner of town since her arrival.

The procession halted while people arranged their pumpkins along the sidewalk. The combined glow transformed the darkened street into something out of a fairy tale, if fairy tales featured severed heads with flames burning inside them.

"Where's Lockie?" Olivia asked.

"He's leading a group of children around the pumpkins, sniffing each one for tokens. He's amassed quite the following. With Mrs. Applewood being the keeper, they smell like the bakery. That's easy for a cat to track."

"There's Rowe." Wally inclined his head toward a figure across the square, behind Councilman Dean and the sheriff.

The pumpkin glow cast harsh shadows across the podcaster's sharp features, transforming her from professional to predatory.

"She's tuned into Dean's distaste for the museum. Her podcast thrives on drama. The contempt's practically written on his face," Wally said.

"Since when do you listen to podcasts?" Tammy asked.

"Xander got me hooked. The true crime stuff fascinates me. How they solve cold cases years later, like we did."

"We should have made a podcast," Olivia said.

"Why didn't I think of that?" Xander slapped his palm against his forehead.

As they rounded the corner, families lined the designated stretch of sidewalk with more pumpkins, creating a breathtaking river of orange light.

Should we extend a warm mug of Spiced Vampire Punch and invite Rowe to join us tonight?

The woman's intensity created an invisible barrier that screamed "keep your distance." Still...

"See you in a bit." She broke away from her friends, propelled by an impulse.

"Ms. Harvey?" Olivia approached, her smile stretching tight across her face. "Enjoying the walk?"

Rowe's gaze flicked up, sharp and assessing. "Just observing. Getting a sense of Willowcroft's... traditions."

"Care to join us?" Olivia gestured to Wally, Tammy, and Xander. "Experience the town from a different perspective, as part of the community?"

Rowe's smile appeared and vanished in an instant, polite but frigid. "Thank you, but I have notes to organize this evening. Early start."

"Tomorrow is Halloween." Why won't she stop digging? What more could she possibly need to know?

"All the more reason to be prepared," Rowe replied, her attention drifting back to the glowing pumpkin path, something calculating in her expression. "Tomorrow will be... enthralling."

Chapter 6

Rainbow threads caught the light as Hazel adjusted her shawl, a small armor against the chill of the tunnel entrance. The main display room teemed with Willow-Crafters assisting with preview day.

"Welcome to the Willowcroft Tunnels Museum!" Pride swelled in her chest as she checked another ticket.

The woman stood ramrod straight, recorder clenched like a weapon. "I'm Rowe Harvey, a true crime podcast host covering today's preview." She thrust her ticket forward, eyes dissecting everything in sight.

Perfect. The vulture arrives right on schedule.

"Ah, yes. We're so pleased you're documenting our town's fascinating history." Hazel kept her voice warm, a practiced defense. "I'm Mrs. Temperance. Do you have any questions for me before your tour?"

Rowe's gaze darted past her, hunting for something. The exhibition tableau stretched behind them with objects found when clearing out the tunnel in preparation for the museum. Everything from moonshine stills to rusted speakeasy tokens was displayed alongside sepia photographs telling stories of an era long past.

Rowe stalked toward the portraits illuminated by amber light. Mary and Cathy stared back from their frames, their love story frozen in time. Between them sat a copy of the bank heist newspaper clipping.

"Quite the tale?" Rowe's words cut through the reverent museum hush.

Hazel moved beside her. "Tragic. Two young lives, intertwined and ended by greed and intolerance."

"Let's talk about that." Rowe positioned her recorder between them without asking permission. Her stare predatory. "Tell me, how did Willowcroft reconcile with this grim chapter of its past?"

Heat ascended Hazel's neck. *Stay calm. Don't give her ammunition.*

"Reconciliation is an ongoing process." She gestured toward Mary and Cathy's images, their faces as familiar to her now as family. "We honor their memory by acknowledging our history, by learning from it. Their love, not the scandal, defines their legacy here now."

"Yet it took decades for the truth to surface." Accusation threaded every word. Rowe's eyes hardened. "Why now after all these years?"

We had no choice once the body was found. Because the town voted. Because not all of us wanted to bury the past.

Hazel met Rowe's challenge head-on. "Sometimes it takes excavation to unearth the truth, literal or otherwise."

Rowe stepped closer, invading Hazel's space. The podcaster reeked of coffee and city perfume. "Was there any resistance to the museum? To exposing the underbelly of Willowcroft's history?" The questions hit rapid-fire, aimed to provoke.

If she wants conflict, she can hunt for it herself.

"Change always meets resistance." Hazel gripped her shawl tighter, the threads tangling between her fingers. "But understanding our past paves the way for a better future. That's what we hope to achieve here."

"Hope." Rowe spat the word like poison. "An optimistic concept for such a sordid tale."

This woman thinks she'll break me with her city cynicism.

"Optimistic, perhaps, but necessary," said Hazel. "Without hope, we remain in darkness. And Willowcroft has spent enough time there, don't you think?"

Rowe's mouth twisted into something not quite a smile. Her fingers stabbed at her recorder, shutting it off with a decisive click. Her eyes darted toward the tunnel entrance.

"Thank you, Mrs. Temperance." She strode away without waiting for a response, her trench coat flapping behind her like wings.

She didn't get what she came for. But she'll be back. That woman won't stop until she's stripped us bare.

The Rowe Harvey whirlwind disappeared into the tunnels with the next tour.

Wally guided the group of journalists deeper into the underground passages. Thirty years of homicide work taught him to read a room. This one reeked of hidden sins.

"...and this section we believe was used to store contraband liquor smuggled in from Canada." He directed the light toward a small cavern, revealing a broken barrel with a faded Canadian logo. "It's easy to take history for granted. But these tunnels are a window into the past. We should appreciate that."

The tour group moved in a tight cluster. Tammy pointed out the chisel marks on the walls while Xander handled questions about the interactive map.

The group halted at a section blocked by wooden barricades and yellow caution tape.

"Parts of the tunnels are still unsafe," Xander said, giving his glasses a quick push. "We're working to reinforce them and hope to access more areas in the future."

A flash of movement caught Wally's eye. That podcaster woman, Rowe Harvey, moved through the crowd with the cold focus of someone casing a scene. Her posture reminded him of perps who thought they were smarter than the detective interviewing them.

"Haven't you investigated them?" Her question sliced through the reverent murmurs of the group. Her stare fixed on the barricades, hungry and calculating. "What are you keeping from the public?"

She's fishing. Thomas warned us.

"History isn't a crime." Wally kept his tone measured, the same cadence he'd once used on suspects who thought charm could cover lies. His grip firmed around the flashlight. "We preserve what we can and respect what we mustn't disturb."

"Even if it means leaving truths buried?" Her lips curled into something between a smile and a sneer.

Two can play this game, Ms. Harvey.

"Especially then." He delivered the words with the calm precision of a man who'd sat across from killers and knew better than to blink. "The past needs proper context. Something real journalists understand."

Rowe stepped closer, her recorder jutting forward. "Interesting stance for a detective with your... track record." Her eyes glinted in the dim light. "Ten years as sheriff here, and you never once stumbled upon these tunnels? Never solved the Mary Collins case? Amateur sleuths saved the day."

The words stung like salt in an old wound. His jaw locked. It had never occurred to him that there were cold cases in the archives.

"Or perhaps that's why you left Homicide?" She pitched her voice low, just for him. "Small-town sheriff seemed safer."

Heat crept over his neck. The memories of his career in Boston and what his family had to endure came flooding back.

He gestured for the group to continue, guiding them toward the next exhibit. Years in interrogation rooms had taught him when to end conversations.

She knows something. Or thinks she does.

Tammy continued the narrative, explaining how bootleggers had created an elaborate warning system using the town's electrical grid. The tour ate it up, but Wally's attention remained divided.

The podcaster lingered at the barricade, her fingers tracing the edge of the caution tape. Close enough to study the scene, far enough to feign innocence. Classic perp behavior. *What are you hunting for?*

The tour moved on, but Wally kept her in the corner of his eye. A prickle crawled up the back of his neck, the same warning that had kept him alive during a drug bust in '98. This wasn't the usual reporter stirring the pot for clicks. No, this one had the look of someone who left damage in her wake and called it justice.

She has no idea what's buried in these tunnels. Neither do they.

Chapter 7

Electricity flowed through ancient wires, bringing 1920s ingenuity back to life beneath Xander's fingertips. The thrill of technology meeting history never got old.

Xander hung back, counting heads and monitoring the signal strength on his custom-built sensor array disguised as a normal flashlight, ensuring his interactive map was working. Six journalists, two tour guides, and one annoying podcaster who kept glancing at her phone.

Probably recording everything.

"Check this out." He flicked a hidden switch he'd restored, sending power through decades-old wiring. Soft amber light bloomed along the tunnel walls, illuminating the path ahead. "Pretty clever for the 1920s, huh?"

His audience murmured appreciatively. A small ping of satisfaction lit him up, like hitting enter and watching a flawless line of code come to life.

"Resourceful," Rowe said, her voice moving closer. She'd fallen back from the main group, positioning herself next to him. Her recorder pointed at his face like a gun. "And you're sure this tech is safe?"

Does she think I'm an amateur?

Xander adjusted his glasses, a nervous habit he couldn't break despite his father's coaching. "I've checked and double-checked everything."

Rowe's lips twitched into what might have been a smile on anyone else. On her, it came across as predatory. "Confident. But confidence has been the downfall of many before you."

She's trying to trip me up. Like those bullies in school.

"Guess I'll have to be the exception." He shrugged, focusing on his tablet instead of her piercing sneer. The code he'd written last night needed tweaking, as did the third bulb flickering at 0.02 seconds off rhythm.

"With these technical skills of yours," Rowe invaded his space, "have you ever snuck into any of these closed-off areas or sent a drone or something in?"

How does she know about the drone?

His fingers twitched toward his pocket where the mini-controller sat. He masked it with a mischievous grin, channeling his radio persona. "I plead the fifth. But seriously, we respect the decision to keep certain passages off-limits until they are safe to explore and study."

Rowe's eyes narrowed, her recorder now inches from his face. "As a teenager, shouldn't you be out with friends instead of burying yourself in technology and tunnels?"

A barb designed to hurt, aimed with precision at his most vulnerable spot. His chest tightened.

Has she stalked my social media?

"What's this I hear about you being a comic? Are you hiding because you failed at that?"

Heat crawled up his neck at the memory of his comedy set. The producer had called it "breakthrough talent."

She's fishing.

"I'll have you know—" His voice cracked, betraying him at the worst possible time.

Wally's baritone boomed from ahead, cutting through the tension. "Okay, folks, let's keep it moving before we turn into bats or vampires or something."

Laughter rippled through the group, chasing off the awkwardness. Rowe stepped back, victory gleaming in her eyes.

She got what she wanted. A reaction. And on tape too.

Xander's fingers strayed to his phone, where a single tap triggered an emergency exit protocol he'd built—a sudden "power failure" forcing evacuation. Tempting.

Instead, he swallowed the hurt and slipped his game face back on. Mom always said the best revenge was success.

"All right, folks, keep close and mind your step." Tammy's voice bounced between the narrow walls. The tour group huddled closer, eyes wide with fascination. Except for Ms. Harvey, whose gaze dissected everything with surgical precision.

"What can you tell us about this section?" Rowe thrust her recorder forward, its red light glaring like an accusation.

She's digging for drama.

"We call this the 'Speakeasy Stretch.'" Tammy gestured toward the bare rock passage, weathered by time. "During Prohibition, these tunnels were a lifeline for those seeking a good time away from prying eyes."

"Sounds romantic," Rowe quipped. "Or desperate."

Don't take the bait. She wants a reaction.

"Depends on your view of romance, I suppose." Tammy maintained her smile, letting the barb slide past her defenses.

Wally and Xander led the group around a corner, their voices fading into the darkness. Rowe lingered behind, her eyes fixed on a section marked "Off-Limits."

If I give her an exclusive, she may back off.

"I'll take you into one of the closed-off sections if you'd like." Tammy lowered her voice, conspiratorial. "But we'll have to be quick. We don't want the others to notice we're gone."

Rowe's eyes sparked with interest, like a predator scenting blood.

They ducked under the caution tape. The temperature plummeted five degrees. Water dripped around them. Tammy swept her flashlight over crumbling walls and debris scattered across the stone floor.

"Watch your step." She stepped over a fallen support beam. "These areas haven't passed the safety checks yet."

Rowe advanced with purpose, recorder extended. "What happened here?"

Show her how much we've discovered, not how much we're hiding.

Tammy launched into historical facts and colorful anecdotes about bootleggers and their coded messages. The tales flowed.

"And the murders? What did the tunnels tell you about Mary Collins or Cathy Robinson?" Rowe cut through the history lesson, zeroing in on her target.

She doesn't care about the tunnels. She wants blood and scandal.

"Parts of their story remain unclear." Tammy weighed each word before speaking. "The tunnels may hold answers."

She directed her flashlight toward a barely visible etching of a crude lantern.

"We're still deciphering the symbols and an old map we have. But not every tunnel is marked, and some sections seem older than Prohibition.

We don't know what they were used for prior to then. There's so much still waiting to be uncovered."

A red laser beam bounced off the wall as Lockie darted past, his collar reflector catching the beam. He wound between Tammy's legs, tail high in greeting. The world's tiniest bodyguard, reporting for duty.

"This is Lockie. He sticks with me through every twist and turn."

The cat sniffed Rowe's boots, whiskers twitching in evaluation before he dashed into the shadows.

"He alerted us to the map and Cathy's remains. He's part of the team."

"Seems like he's got the right owner." Her tone teased, but her eyes remained sharp, assessing.

What game is she playing?

They rejoined the primary route. Tammy directed her light toward a wooden door with a pestle-and-mortar symbol scratched into the frame. "This marked the way to the old apothecary. Now it leads to the Swinging Spoon diner and marks the end of the tour."

"Prohibition-era signage." She snapped a photo with her phone. "Clever."

They emerged through the door set into the diner's basement wall. On the opposite side, Tammy pointed out the cocktail etching, a silent invitation to those seeking forbidden pleasures.

"What is it like to have such a remarkable piece of history right in your backyard?" Rowe asked.

"Unreal." The word escaped before Tammy could dress it up. "Every day, I discover something new and exciting about Willowcroft's past. It's been an incredible journey so far."

"So, you left LA for... this? Why?" Rowe's question sliced through the pleasantries.

My escape. My sanctuary.

"Sometimes the quietest places have the loudest voices." Tammy crafted the line with care. "And I've always loved mysteries."

"Even your own?" Rowe stepped closer.

Tammy met her gaze. "Especially my own."

"Anything you couldn't solve? Maybe something from your career?"

Does she know about the stolen manuscript? How could she?

Her stomach constricted. Dom and Sally had taken every file and note, leaving Tammy with no proof she'd ever written the masterpiece now bearing Sally's name. The book wasn't even in stores yet. Only the three of them knew the truth.

No way Rowe knows.

"Tell me more about Cathy and Mary's story. What do you think drove them to rob the bank?"

"They were desperate for a life together," Tammy said, settling into firmer ground. "They dreamed of escaping small-town limits and finding acceptance in the city. The stolen money was their ticket to freedom."

The fluorescent lights of the diner assaulted her eyes as they emerged from the tunnel. Chrome bar stools gleamed beneath vintage fixtures. A jukebox played soft music from another era. Peggy stood ready at the counter, lips curved in a welcoming smile that masked her sharp business sense.

"Welcome back, folks! Ten percent off for museum ticket holders. And I've got a cherry pie that'll make you forget every trouble you ever had."

"Thanks." Tammy's shoulders relaxed in the familiar surroundings.

"Sit anywhere you like, darlin'." Peggy's attention fixed on Rowe with recognition. "Ms. Harvey. I've listened to your podcast. I never dreamed I'd see you in my diner."

She slid into the seat across from Rowe while pouring coffee with practiced ease. "Imagine if I'd said no to them exploring downstairs. We never would have found the tunnels and poor Cathy."

Rowe leaned forward, a hand clasped around her mug, recorder pointed at Peggy like a weapon. "That must have been quite a shock for the town."

"Honey, it was like the world turned upside down for a minute there." Peggy sighed. "But you know what they say about tragedy bringing people together. We're a stronger community now because of it."

"Or it exposes secrets some might prefer stayed buried." Rowe's voice hardened.

Always digging. Always pushing.

"Secrets?" Peggy laughed, genuine and warm. She winked at Rowe. "Oh, everyone has those! But in Willowcroft, we like to think our skeletons are more interesting than most."

"The town seems like a tight-knit place. Everyone involved, everyone affected. Tunnels running beneath your feet like veins through the heart of the community."

"Exactly like that," Peggy agreed. "And like veins, they keep life pumping through us. History isn't just about the past, Ms. Harvey. It's alive, shaping us right now. And who knows what else we might uncover?"

"Thanks for the coffee and the insight." Rowe stood, gathering her recorder and notebook.

"Anytime, hon. And remember, secrets in small towns are like seeds. You never know when they'll sprout again."

Rowe departed, her trademark trench coat swinging with each step. Whatever the woman was seeking, she wouldn't stop until she found it. *What happens when she does?*

Chapter 8

Coffee sloshed inside Tammy's travel mug as she crossed the field from the little blue cottage to the tunnel entrance, keys swinging in one hand. The November morning air bit at her cheeks while forgotten jack-o'-lanterns from Halloween eve sat along the grassy path. Some had collapsed inward. Others still bore mischievous grins.

She paused at the door, noting hardened candle wax, reddish smudges on the handle, and scratches around the keyhole. The OPENING NOVEMBER 1 sign hung in place. Today was the grand launch after months of work.

Tammy inserted the key, but it was unlocked. She pushed the door, fumbled for the light switch, and froze.

Her mug slipped from her fingers. Scalding coffee splashed Tammy's shoes and legs as the cup tumbled down the steps with hollow thuds. The remaining liquid pooled at the bottom.

Rowe Harvey lay crumpled at the base of the staircase, recorder in hand, one earbud tangled in a spill of dark hair. The woman's face was a frozen mask of terror. A dried trickle of blood stained the corner of her mouth.

Mrs. Hubbard's decorative owl pumpkin perched on a ledge behind the figure, its carved eyes staring vacantly into the gloom.

Tammy's stomach lurched. Her legs went numb. She'd seen death before—Cathy's bones in the tunnels, black-and-white photos of Mary's corpse—but never like this. Never someone she had talked to yesterday.

Her first real experience with death. The first time it had a name and a voice she remembered.

Tammy stumbled backward, her lungs refusing to work. Trembling fingers fumbled for her phone as she staggered outside into the cold morning.

Sheriff Stanton arrived with his team. Two officers strung yellow tape across the entrance while Stanton approached Tammy, who stood shivering on the museum steps.

"Miss Rumbelow. Show me where the body is, please?"

Tammy swallowed hard, her throat tight. She led him through the entrance, past the pooled coffee from the shattered mug. Each step toward the scene clenched her stomach tighter.

"There," she said, pointing.

Stanton crossed the threshold, and his posture stiffened as his eyes fixed on Rowe's crumpled form at the base of the stairs.

"It's Rowe Harvey." Tammy forced herself to peek at the body. The second viewing brought the same jolt of horror. "True crime podcaster. She interviewed people connected to the tunnels and museum. Our team, Peggy Hughes, even the Willow-Crafters."

Stanton rubbed the back of his neck. "I'll need to speak with everyone on that list. But those Crafter ladies will drown me in tea before I get a straight answer." His lips twitched in a failed attempt at levity.

"I only opened the door. Touched nothing. The coffee's mine."

"Anyone else here?"

"No."

The image of Rowe's body flashed through Tammy's mind again. Her stomach twisted. This wasn't like finding bones, studying old case files, or writing about a murder. The cold had settled in, but the horror still felt fresh.

Time slowed as a realization washed over her. "Sheriff," she said, her voice unsteady. "We're all suspects now, aren't we? The entire team?"

He paused, his face grim. "I'll interview everyone connected to this museum. Evidence will guide us. But right now, you're my primary person of interest."

Tammy's hands clenched. "I'll cooperate fully. But most of us live alone, except for me and Lockie." She glanced down at her cat.

Stanton didn't laugh, but his silence did the smirking for him. "Your cat is your alibi?"

"I'm his. We stayed home last night. We're too far out for trick-or-treaters apart from one early group."

The sheriff scribbled in his notebook. "I'll consider that, but expect further questions about your whereabouts. Maybe Lockie will need to give a statement too." The corner of his mouth lifted.

"Sure." Tammy's gaze drifted back to the museum entrance. Her fingers tingled with numbness as the reality settled in. A woman she'd spoken with yesterday lay dead. A woman whose probing behavior had irritated the whole town. Whose recorder had captured Willowcroft's sounds and secrets.

"Cancel today's opening," Stanton said. "Then meet me at the Sheriff's Department... And Miss Rumbelow?" His stare hardened. "No amateur sleuthing."

Tammy nodded, her eyes fixed on the yellow crime scene tape rippling in the breeze. A sight far too familiar since she'd relocated. Their grand opening, months of work and anticipation, now buried beneath a murder investigation with her at its center.

Sleuthing was the farthest thing from her mind. Her brain shifted into damage control. The Waves of Willowcroft radio station could announce the cancellation on their morning show. Olivia had to be told. She had the contacts to cancel the shuttle bus. And Mrs. T could mobilize the Willow-Crafters to spread the word, especially to Katie at Mrs. Hubbard's Cupboard, the fastest news pipeline in town.

The day stretched before her, transformed from celebration to crisis management in a single, horrifying discovery.

"I imagine being a prime suspect is quite involved," she muttered to herself.

Olivia's going to love this!

Chapter 9

The Sheriff's Department pulsed with unease. Tammy sat on the hard wooden bench, Lockie curled on her lap, his tail swaying in sharp, irritated arcs. Olivia, Wally, Mrs. Temperance, and Xander surrounded her in a jittery line of sleuths-turned-suspects, shifting uncomfortably in the too-quiet waiting area.

The air reeked of burnt coffee. Somewhere behind the closed doors, a phone rang and rang, unanswered.

She rubbed clammy palms against her jeans, then clasped them tight to stop the shaking. Lockie meowed as she shifted. Across the room, Wally picked at a loose thread on his sleeve. Olivia chewed her bottom lip. Xander slouched deeper in his seat. Mrs. T muttered something under her breath—not intended for sensitive ears.

"Stanton's just doing his job," Olivia whispered, sounding like she was convincing herself. "I've never had to put a sign on the door saying 'Closed because of being a murder suspect.'"

Tammy scratched behind her cat's ears, her thoughts stuck on the image of Rowe. Still. Silent. Gone. Not just a name in an old case file.

"Feels like we're the ones on trial," she said.

"We should've dressed as prisoners for Halloween," Xander said under his breath. The joke fell flat.

"Everything's going to be fine," Mrs. T added, though even she sounded unsure. "We need to stick together."

Sheriff Stanton approached, clipboard in hand, expression unreadable.

"All right," he said, voice clipped. "Who's first?"

Tammy sighed, nudging Lockie off her lap. "Let's get it over with."

She followed the sheriff into a cramped room with mint green walls and a metal table bolted to the floor. A single fluorescent light hummed overhead.

"Sit." He gestured to a plastic chair.

She settled into the seat, which squeaked under her weight.

Stanton sat opposite and placed his clipboard on the table. "Let's start from the beginning. What time did you arrive at the museum this morning?"

"Just before seven."

He scribbled something on his paper. "And you were the first there?"

"Yes." The image of Rowe's body flashed through her mind again. She pressed her palms flat to the cold table.

"Who has keys to the museum?"

"Me, Olivia, Wally, and Mrs. Temperance."

Stanton's pen scratched against the paper. "When was the last time you saw Rowe Harvey alive?"

"Yesterday afternoon. She interviewed me about the museum after a tour around two." Tammy's mouth went dry.

"What was your relationship with the victim?"

Tammy shifted in her seat. "Professional. We only met yesterday. Rowe asked questions; I answered them."

"Was she concerned about anything? Frightened?"

"No. Her only focus was getting under my skin."

"Did she threaten you?"

"No. But her questioning was designed to spark a reaction from me."

Stanton leaned forward. "What did she ask you about?"

"The history of the tunnels. Cathy's skeleton. She wanted access to the cordoned-off areas."

"And what did you tell her?"

"The truth." She picked at a hangnail on her thumb. "Everyone in town talked to her. She was digging into Willowcroft's secrets. People don't like that."

"People like who?"

Tammy hesitated. "The Willow-Crafters, Peggy, other business owners, Council members, Thomas at the Gazette."

"Did you like her?"

The question caught her off guard. "I respected her work."

"That's not what I asked."

"She was persistent. Annoyingly so." Tammy took a deep breath. "But I barely knew her, so I had no reason to wish her harm."

Stanton tapped his pen against the table. "Tell me about your movements yesterday evening."

"After the last preview tour, I had a quick early dinner with the team at Swinging Spoon about five, then headed home. I checked that the museum was locked, then relaxed before the grand opening today by watching a new mystery show with Lockie."

"Alone? Besides the cat?"

"Yes."

"No phone calls? Visitors?"

"Mrs. Hubbard's grandkids came by for trick-or-treating soon after I got back around six. Then nothing until this morning. I'm too far out for mainstream trick-or-treating."

Stanton jotted something down. "What time did you go to bed?"

"By ten."

"And between six and ten, you never left your house?"

"No."

"You know how this looks? No witnesses, no alibi."

A vise gripped Tammy's chest. "I understand."

Stanton's next question came quickly enough that she didn't have time to dwell on that fact.

"You found the museum unlocked?"

"Yes. There were scratches around the keyhole. I had a key, so I didn't need to pick the lock and create marks."

"You could have faked them to take suspicion off yourself."

That should have got me off the hook. "It wasn't me."

"And the security cameras?"

"We haven't installed any yet. We didn't consider them a priority with the quick timeline."

The sheriff glared at her.

Her stomach dropped. "I swear I was home all night."

"Did you see Ms. Harvey using any equipment besides the recorder?"

"I saw the microphone she waved at everyone."

Stanton's pen paused mid-scratch. "Let's talk about the pumpkin."

"The pumpkin?"

"Mrs. Hubbard's owl pumpkin. It was found at the scene."

"What about it?"

"Did you notice anything unusual about it?"

"I saw it sitting there."

The room suddenly felt too small, too hot. "I don't understand where you're going with this."

"I'm suggesting someone placed it there. Someone who knew Mrs. Hubbard had distributed those pumpkins around town."

"Including to me, to signal my house as a safe place for trick-or-treaters." *Does he think I put it there after the trick-or-treaters?* "But I didn't expect any trick-or-treaters, so I left mine at the museum to add to the Halloween vibe."

Stanton made another note. "Sure."

"I found a body. I didn't create one."

"That's what we're here to determine." He stood. "We'll be processing the scene for several days. The museum remains closed until further notice."

"What happens now?"

"I talk to your friends out there." He gestured toward the waiting area. "And you stay in town, Ms. Rumbelow. No travel plans."

"One question, Sheriff. How did she die?"

Stanton paused. "The medical examiner hasn't reported the cause of death yet."

"But it wasn't an accident? As in a fall down the stairs?"

His expression hardened. "Someone wanted her dead. And the evidence is pointing straight at you."

A sharp knock interrupted them. Deputy Brown burst in, breathless.

"Sheriff, you need to see this." He clutched a stack of manila folders against his chest. "We found these at the Willowcroft Inn where Harvey was staying."

Stanton's eyes narrowed. "What have you got?"

"Dossiers, sir." He placed the stack on the table. "She had files on half the town. The top one is especially useful right now."

Tammy's gaze dropped to the new evidence. Her own name stood out in bold black marker on the top file.

Stanton flipped open the cover as he sat, his eyebrows rising as he scanned the first page. "Interesting timing, Deputy."

She counted at least ten in the pile. More people than just the team. Rowe had cast a wide net.

While the sheriff thumbed through her file, Tammy strained to see the labels on the other folders. The edge of one slipped into sight—Olivia written in the same scrawl. Another peeked out with Wallace scrawled across its tab. She caught a glimpse of what looked like "Evan" on one before Stanton shifted the pile, blocking her view.

"We've found a motive."

"Multiple motives, I would say," retorted Tammy.

"These change things," Stanton said, closing her file and tapping it with his index finger. "Ms. Harvey was conducting quite the investigation into townsfolk."

"She's a true crime podcaster. Investigating is her job." Tammy slouched back. "Was her job."

"This goes beyond podcast research." Stanton slid the stack away from her. "These are methodical. Personal. Like blackmail material."

The fluorescent light buzzed above them. Tammy's throat went dry.

"What's in my file?"

She can't know. She can't... She shook it off, reminding herself Sally and Dom were in the wrong, not her. *I'm the victim.*

Stanton stood, gathering the folders. "In light of these, we'll have more questions for you later."

Tammy's stomach knotted. "I'm not your only suspect anymore, am I?"

"You're still at the top of my list." Stanton nodded to Brown. "But it just got longer."

The deputy held the door open. "What about the others?"

"Ascertain their alibis, then send them home. We can call them back in after I go through the dossiers."

"Already done, sir," said Deputy Brown. "All home alone with no one to vouch for them except young Xander, whose parents confirm he was with them."

The sheriff's jaw tightened. "A town full of loners with no alibis. Great."

Tammy pushed herself up from the chair. "Can I go too?"

"For now." Stanton's focus lingered on her face. "But don't play detective."

She squeezed past them into the hallway, the weight of their stares pressing against her back. *A true crime writer with secret files. A body in her museum. And the sheriff is focusing on an owl pumpkin.*

This was definitely a job for the team.

Who in Willowcroft had killed to keep their secrets?

She joined the others in the waiting area, but before they left, Stanton called out, "One more thing."

The group turned as one.

"If any of you come across new information—anything—bring it straight to me. No detours. No stunts."

"Understood," Olivia said, her tone measured.

The sheriff gave a short nod and returned to his desk, already buried in the files.

Tammy and the others sat in the back room of Bookworm Haven. Lockie perched himself on a stack of museum brochures, blinking as if unimpressed with the lot of them.

"We're doing this, right?" Olivia asked as she took a seat. "We need to clear our names. Being alone for your alibi doesn't help anyone."

Tammy folded her arms. "Lockie was there."

"I'll make sure he takes the stand," Wally said with a faint smirk.

"Better than some humans I know," Mrs. T said, earning a tired laugh.

Xander tapped a rhythm on the tabletop. "Stanton's convinced we're hiding something. We'll have to prove we're not."

"And to do that," Olivia said, straightening her glasses, "we have to find the murderer."

They sat in silence for a beat.

"Rowe poked a lot of bears," Wally said.

"And one of them snapped," Mrs. T replied.

"We need to retrace her steps," Olivia suggested. "Who she spoke to. What she might have discovered." Her expression changed to pure delight as she continued. "Time for the murder board."

Eye rolls spread around the room. *Only Olivia can be excited about such a thing.*

Olivia had disappeared into the main store before returning with the board they had used for their previous two investigations. Where in the store it lived was still a mystery.

The door to the back room, disguised as a bookshelf sitting between the true crime and esoteric sections, wasn't the only thing hidden in the building.

"When do you think I should book Mike in to fix the window in case he gets busy?" was the first thing Olivia said upon her return, her voice a touch too casual to be believable.

Tammy fought back a smile. Olivia wasn't fooling anyone.

"Just because your storefront has been broken three times during our investigations doesn't mean it will happen again," said Mrs. T.

"You want it to though so you get to ogle Mike," Xander teased, his expression pure teenage mischief as he waggled his eyebrows like two caterpillars doing the salsa. "Breaking news: Local bookstore owner considering vandalism of own property to see the hot glazier!"

"You could simply call him and ask him out," Wally said with blunt practicality. "Save yourself the insurance premium hike."

Olivia recoiled, hands flying up as if someone had suggested she read the last page of a mystery novel first. "Not a chance. How do I know how he feels about me? I might be nothing more than another customer."

"You're more than a regular old customer," said Xander, his grin spreading wider. "You're a frequent flyer. I think you've earned enough Mike Miles for a free dinner date."

Tammy joined in. "I've never seen anyone so fascinated by glass installation techniques. The way you watch him while he works, making moon faces at him..." She mimicked the dreamy expression she'd caught on Olivia's face during Mike's last visit.

"I do not! I don't know what any of you are talking about!" Olivia protested, gripping the murder board so tightly her knuckles whitened.

The blush creeping up Olivia's neck and flooding her cheeks was as entertaining as the denials. Tammy bit her lip to keep from laughing too hard as everyone chuckled around them.

"I was being efficient and planning ahead," Olivia insisted, her voice climbing higher with each word.

"Don't these things happen in threes?" asked Wally. "Well then, you're off the hook. First the bear, then the brick, followed by a toddler tantrum.

I think you're safe... until you accidentally-on-purpose drop something heavy near the display window."

Olivia turned to Tammy with a desperate glance, begging for rescue. As much as Tammy enjoyed the rare sight of her confident friend flustered, she threw her a lifeline.

"Let's assign tasks," she said, drawing everyone's attention. "If we all dig, we'll cover more ground."

The relief on Olivia's face was clear as she seized the change in conversation like a drowning woman grabbing a life preserver.

"Tammy, you and Lockie go back to the museum and check out what's happening at the crime scene. Use binoculars if you can't get close enough."

Tammy nodded but filed away this Mike situation for future teasing opportunities.

"Mrs. T," Wally said, "chat with the Willow-Crafters. They'll have the latest news from Mrs. Hubbard's Cupboard."

"I'll dig through Rowe's socials and online presence," Xander offered. "She might've hinted at something she found."

"I'll talk to Peggy," Olivia said. "And other local businesses too."

"I'll swing by the inn," Wally added. "The manager might know her comings and goings."

A quiet spark lit in Tammy's chest. They had a plan.

"We'll meet back here tonight," Olivia said, rising to her feet. "Compare notes and share everything."

So much for an opening day.

They were hunting a killer instead. And a present-day one at that.

Chapter 10

Wally stepped into the Willowcroft Inn, his boots leaving muddy prints on the orange-and-black rug as he scraped off leaves clinging to his soles. The place held the faint scent of roasted marshmallows from the inn's firepit the night before, mixed with nutmeg-scented potpourri and a lingering trace of costume glue.

Outside, Mrs. Hubbard's distinctive owl pumpkin sat guard on the front step. Now it served as a grim reminder of how quickly Halloween had transformed from celebration to crime scene.

"Afternoon, George," Wally said, tipping an imaginary hat as he stepped up to the reception desk. "Hope you survived the sugar stampede."

The innkeeper peered up from a stack of Halloween-themed check-in forms, his spiderweb-printed bowtie crooked. "Wallace. If I see another foam sword or glitter cape today, I'm retiring to a monastery."

Wally chuckled. "Your wife, Georgina, might have something to say about that. I have a quick question."

"More sleuthing?"

"I'm pinning down Rowe Harvey's movements last night." Wally pulled out his pocket notebook. The one with a corner chewed off by his grandson's new puppy last month. "What time did she leave?"

George rubbed his stubbled chin. "It was right when my Halloween playlist hit 'Monster Mash' for the second time. I remember because I'd reset it at six, and that song plays every thirty minutes."

"Seven then?"

"Thereabouts." George leaned in. "Strangest thing, though, she had not long returned and ordered pizza. Delivery guy from Pizza Pasta Palooza showed up ten minutes after she bolted."

Wally paused mid-scribble. "She ordered food, then immediately left?"

"Paid for it, too. Told me to enjoy it." George shook his head. "That pizza had everything on it. Twenty-five bucks down the drain if she wasn't coming back."

"How'd she seem when she left?"

"Frantic. Phone pinged, she checked it, then rushed straight for the door." George mimed pushing through a crowd. "Bowled over those kids dressed as the Addams Family. The little Wednesday gave her such a glare. If looks could kill, Wednesday would be our prime suspect."

Wally underlined the time in his notebook, the first concrete marker in Rowe's final hours. Who texts someone at seven on Halloween night that makes them abandon a prepaid pizza?

"Did she say where she was going?"

"Not a word. She pushed past the trick-or-treaters, knocked over my skeleton butler, and vanished." George tapped his fingers on the counter.

Wally's instincts tingled. He rolled the pen between his fingers to steady his thoughts. Rowe wouldn't have ordered food if she planned to leave. Whatever that message was, she thought it mattered more than pizza. She'd rushed out chasing something urgent, maybe a breakthrough. But she hadn't seen the danger in it. Not then. Not until it was too late.

Hazel settled into her armchair, the pom-poms on her shawl swaying like little tasseled ghosts as she poured tea from her best china pot. The Willow-Crafters gathered around her coffee table, drawn by warm scones, buttery jam, and the irresistible lure of gossip.

"Ladies, I know we're all shaken by the news of poor Rowe's passing," she said.

"Cold cases are one thing, but an actual murder," Della Mae said, clutching her knitting like it might protect her from further crime. "It's as if Agatha Christie came to Willowcroft wearing a witch's hat and demanded a mug of punch."

"There were so many burglars, ghosts, and ghouls out last night. Who could tell the real from the fake?" said Marjorie, stirring her tea as if it owed her money.

"Was someone burgled?" Betty's eyes fluttered in quick succession.

Marjorie rolled her eyes but kept quiet. For her, that was practically saintly.

"Focus," Hazel said, tapping her spoon twice against her cup. "We must do everything we can to help solve what happened to Ms. Harvey. Think back to anything unusual. Anyone acting strangely. Or who didn't belong."

A thoughtful silence settled over the room, broken only by the dainty clink of teacups and the soft hum of Della Mae's electric foot warmer.

"I saw her with Thomas Berry from the Gazette multiple times," Della Mae offered. "He looked like he'd rather be having a root canal."

"Thomas warned us Rowe was difficult to deal with," Hazel nodded. "Anyone else?"

Beatrice set her teacup down. "I overheard Mrs. Robinson telling Katie at the Cupboard that Rowe was asking about Cathy."

Marjorie harrumphed. "Terrible thing, what happened. But that girl was trouble, poking around with her pesky questions."

"What do you know, Marjorie?" asked Hazel.

"She interrogated Gerald about his father's time on the council. What would Henry Hubbard know about the tunnels? Different time, different circumstances."

Hazel paused, her spoon mid-air. *Odd connection.*

Marjorie shook her head. "She was stirring up too much. Even asked Evan Dean something about council minutes, poor man dropped his candy—"

"And that's when two young girls in princess costumes went head-to-head over the same pumpkin bucket," added Della Mae. "One got so worked up she emptied her stomach onto the petunias as a unicorn lit a marshmallow on fire and flung it like a comet across the square."

"That's right," said Betty. I checked my watch to see if it was six thirty yet to take my medication, which it was, then got distracted by something flying overhead. I thought it was a bat and nearly fainted."

"Then Roger reminded me he wanted chili for dinner at his usual seven, and he expected me to be there with him," said Della Mae.

Roger was so stuck in his ways. Poor Della Mae could never miss serving him dinner at seven on the dot every night. Harold was the unpredictable one in Hazel's marriage, with emergency medical calls and all.

"You know I love Halloween," said Marjorie, "but it brings out the crazies. I saw a grown man in a werewolf mask hanging around the town hall candy table. No kids. Just... loitering. Gave me the shivers."

"I bet the killer was someone in disguise," Betty said. "No one would pay any attention to an ax murderer walking down the street that night!"

"You've been watching too many murder mysteries," Beatrice muttered, passing the plate of scones again.

Hazel forced a smile as the chatter rolled on. Betty was right. It was the perfect night to commit a murder with no one noticing.

Yellow tape fluttered in the fall breeze as forensic techs moved like ants through the field outside the museum. Tammy stood beyond the perimeter, arms folded against the cold. The Michigan chill seeped through the seams of her coat, a far cry from the sun-soaked Octobers of Los Angeles.

Lockie wove between her legs, his tail cutting through the air in restless sweeps.

Deputies held the line, a wall of uniforms guarding the scene. Getting any closer would only paint a bigger target on her back. From here, the occasional word floated past. Each one was muffled, out of context, and impossible to stitch into anything useful.

But the wind shifted and carried a sentence toward her.

"Phone's missing. Not at the inn, not in the rental car, not here."

The killer must have it.

Tammy hadn't associated Rowe with a phone. It was always the recorder in her hand, red light blinking while she asked her pointed questions. So why would someone take the phone and leave the recorder?

Unless it wasn't the interviews they were worried about, but something else they wanted to erase.

Olivia had been inundated with inquiries about the museum closure, leaving her trapped behind the counter while her investigation stalled.

Making the most of a lull, she fired off a quick text:

Olivia: Can I meet you on the stoop?

Peggy: Sure thing, honey.

Olivia slipped outside and waited.

The door of the Swinging Spoon swung open, and Peggy emerged in her coffee-splashed apron.

"Hello, darlin', what's up?"

"I'm piecing together Rowe's movements before her death. Did she stop by the diner yesterday?"

"She chatted with Tammy after the tunnel tour, then came back later." Peggy lowered her voice. "Seemed antsy, kept scanning the door and checking her watch."

"Was she meeting someone?"

"If she was, they never showed." Peggy wiped her hands. "But she stirred the pot with half my customers. One conversation ended with a fellow storming out without paying his check. Then she bolted herself."

Peggy waved it off. "It didn't seem like anything unusual. People argue in here all the time."

But Olivia wasn't convinced. A customer walking out on a bill and another leaving in a huff? That was more than just diner noise—

Peggy cracked the door to the Swinging Spoon. "They've been at it nonstop. Stick your head in for a minute and hear for yourself."

Olivia leaned in. A jumble of voices spilled out, overlapping and cutting each other off.

"It's always the quiet ones." A gravelly male voice dominated the others. "I'm telling you, that librarian gives me the creeps."

"That's because you owe late fees from 1992," a woman, sharp and quick with her retort.

A higher-pitched voice chimed in, "No, no. It was an out-of-towner. No Willowcrofter would kill a woman over a podcast. That's big-city behavior."

"You think someone drove all the way from Detroit to murder a podcaster in our tunnel museum?" This speaker sounded skeptical, their words dripping with sarcasm.

"Stranger things have happened." The voice reminded Olivia of an old television announcer. "Remember when that Elvis impersonator robbed Mrs. Hubbard's Cupboard?"

"That was your cousin Darryl," came a flat, matter-of-fact tone.

Olivia pulled back from the door, the accusations still ringing in her ears.

"See what I mean?" Peggy whispered. "They're two theories away from forming a pitchfork committee."

"I'll keep my escape route clear."

Peggy returned to the diner while Olivia retreated to the bookstore.

Three tourists poured in, armed with questions about the murder and museum closure. Olivia tucked her notebook away with a sigh.

But after they'd left, she closed down for the day. No one was buying anything except gossip. So why stay open? She'd achieve more away from the store.

She grabbed her coat and headed to the salon, Teased & Polished, across the square.

Hairspray, citrus hand cream, and gossip hung thick in the air as Olivia entered. A blow dryer whirred in the background, mixing with laughter and the clink of nail tools. The familiar low, steady chorus of beauty in progress pulsed through the room.

"Olivia!" called Vanessa, the salon's owner and reigning queen of both highlights and town headlines. "You here for a trim or a rumor?"

"Asking questions," Olivia said, offering a polite smile. "About Rowe Harvey."

The dryer snapped off.

Every head turned.

"Oh," someone by the polish display said, "*her*."

Vanessa gestured toward the empty styling chair near the front. "Take a seat. We were just talking about that woman."

Olivia sat, notebook at the ready. "Did she come in here before… you know?"

Vanessa nodded. "Twice. First time, came in asking for a dry trim but never even took off her hat. Kept poking around about council members, old businesses, anything connected with the tunnels. Said she wanted a 'locals' perspective.'"

"She interviewed my cousin while getting a file and paint," said Bree, the manicurist. "Told her she'd heard the mayor had a secret entrance to the tunnels in his backyard."

"That's ridiculous," Olivia said, amused. "He barely has room for a lawn chair."

"I know," Bree said. "But Ms. Harvey wasn't saying it because she believed it. She was trying to get a reaction. You know, flicking polish to see where it landed."

"She asked me if any of my clients ever came in with dirty shoes and nervous habits," Vanessa added. "I told her the only suspicious thing in this town was how fast we run out of cinnamon at Sweet Crumbs."

"She asked me," said Bree, "if any of my nail clients ever mentioned seeing strange lights near the cemetery. Like I keep a notebook of spooky gossip."

Olivia scribbled notes. "Did she mention any names?"

"Loads," Bree said. "All the councilors. Oh, and she didn't like the Willow-Crafters."

"What?"

Vanessa lowered her voice. "Said they were 'too cozy.' Like their whole knitting meeting was a cover for something. I told her the only thing they're hiding is the blueberry scone recipe, and Mrs. Temperance is right to keep it secret."

That earned a ripple of laughter.

"She made people uncomfortable," Bree said. "She didn't care about the town. Only about what she could tear open."

Olivia nodded. "Thank you. That's helpful."

As she stood to leave, Vanessa called after her, "If you find out she was right about something, don't tell me. I like my mysteries in paperbacks."

Chapter 11

In the cozy confines of Olivia's back room, Xander searched through Rowe's online presence.

Her social media revealed little beyond announcements about her podcast. He clicked over to her website, skimming the episode descriptions. His eyes widened at the sight of her most recent one. She recorded a live show the night she died.

Donning his headphones, he pressed play. Rowe's voice echoed through the museum's dark tunnels, her tone calm. She mentioned finding the door open and entering alone.

Xander tensed as her footsteps stopped.

"Hello? Is someone there?" she called out.

Silence.

A faint rustle of movement.

The clatter of a struggle.

A muffled cry.

Nothing.

Goosebumps prickled his arms.

He yanked off the headphones.

Well, that wasn't creepy much.

He grabbed his phone. His thumbs flew across the screen:

Xander: EVERYONE BACK TO THE BOOKSTORE NOW. FOUND SOMETHING.

He replayed the track, increasing the volume and filtering frequencies, hunting for any background sound that might identify the killer.

"Hey, Xander!" Wally's deep baritone boomed as he walked through the disguised door. "What's up?"

Xander thrust his hand up. "Shush." He adjusted a setting on his audio program, isolating a faint snippet of dialogue.

"Sorry." Wally dropped to a stage whisper and perched on the edge of a chair, its wooden frame creaking.

Olivia burst through the door. "Did you find something?"

Tammy, Lockie, and Mrs. Temperance filed in behind her.

Xander unplugged his headphones. "Listen." He clicked play and cranked the volume.

The recording filled the room. Five pairs of eyes locked onto the laptop as Rowe's last moments played out. Mrs. T pressed her handkerchief to her mouth.

"There's more." Xander minimized the audio program. "I broke into her calendar in the cloud. She had an appointment scheduled at the museum at eight o'clock that night with someone listed only as 'A'."

"Who's 'A'?" Tammy twisted a strand of hair around her finger.

"Working on it." Xander's fingers danced across the keyboard. "I'm hacking her email password now. Give me a sec..."

The others huddled together, trading notes on their investigations. Their voices faded into background noise as he slipped into the familiar comfort of code and keystrokes, but Wally mentioned something about pizza and the meeting being spontaneous.

"Got it!" Xander's triumphant shout silenced the room. "Check this out."

He spun the laptop to display an email chain between Rowe and an encrypted address.

"This 'A' person practically dared her to come here." He highlighted a message and read aloud. "'I have a juicy tale for you, if you think you're brave enough to uncover the truth. A remote town called Willowcroft has secrets buried in its past.'"

Olivia scribbled 'A' on the murder board. "Someone lured her here."

"To kill her," added Mrs. T, clutching her necklace.

"Can you trace the email?" Wally loomed over Xander's shoulder, his breath hot against Xander's neck.

"Back up, big guy. Personal space." He shrugged away from Wally's hovering. "And yeah, I can. The encryption's basic, so it won't take long."

He fired up a program he definitely hadn't downloaded legally and typed a string of commands. The screen filled with scrolling text.

Lockie launched himself onto the table, scattering printouts like digital bits after a system crash. Papers cascaded to the floor, breaking Xander's concentration mid-hack.

Tammy lunged for the cat, missing him by inches.

Xander snatched his laptop away from the chaos. Four-legged interference was the last thing he needed.

"Someone wants to be the center of attention," Wally said.

The cat's tail waved like a victory banner as he surveyed his handiwork. Great. Now the physical files were as disorganized as most people's hard drives.

"Or perhaps he's found a clue we've overlooked." Olivia dropped to her knees, gathering papers while dodging Lockie's batting paw.

Xander rolled his eyes. The others always attributed some master detective skills to the cat.

"Let's get all this back in order—" Tammy stopped mid-sentence as Lockie smacked a pen off the table with feline determination.

"There goes our lead." Xander snorted, focusing back on his screen. The email trace ran in the background, algorithms churning through digital breadcrumbs.

Tammy retrieved the pen, wagging it at her cat. "You scoundrel, you're as much a part of this team as any of us. You don't need theatrics."

Lockie meowed, pawing at the air like he understood. Which he didn't, regardless of what the others believed.

"We can't dismiss his... unique approach," Mrs. T said.

"Unique is one word for it." Olivia scratched behind Lockie's ears. "You're too charming, aren't you?"

Xander refocused on his screen, tuning out the cat appreciation society meeting. The search algorithm crawled through Rowe's online presence, compiling metadata from her social accounts.

"Xander, anything new?" Tammy asked.

"Not yet." His fingers continued their dance across the keyboard.

"We'll go over the podcast with a fine-toothed—" Another pen clattered to the floor, cutting off Tammy's words.

"Lockie! This is serious business."

"Ah, he's living up to his role in our detective agency," Mrs. T said, retrieving the pen. "Every sleuthing team needs a mischief-maker."

"We can't forget the missing phone," Olivia added. "The killer must've taken it, but why?"

"They probably knew she was recording," Wally said.

"Rowe used a separate device though," Tammy said. "And I saw it next to her body."

"How do we have that last podcast then?" Wally asked.

Xander smirked. Such tech illiteracy. "She was live streaming. Automatically uploaded to her podcast channel and the cloud, thanks to my Wi-Fi setup for the museum's interactive maps."

"Technology has come a long way since my time," Mrs. T said.

"And mine," Wally added.

"Maybe she had digital copies of the dossiers Deputy Brown found," said Olivia. "They could've been on her phone."

"Wish we could get our hands on those," Wally muttered as he paced. "Xander, can you access them online?"

"They wouldn't have been digitized yet, if at all."

"What about Bev?" Mrs. T asked.

"No. She has access to the archives, not anything on Stanton's desk."

"Why was Rowe investigating us anyway?" Tammy asked. "How did she get our names for a file in the first place?"

"They were mentioned in the newspapers with the tunnel discovery," said Mrs. T.

Chapter 12

"Let's see what Lockie insisted we discover with all those antics." Tammy glared at the cat, who blinked back with feline indifference. If he existed in her books, he'd be the mischievous sidekick who held crucial clues.

"They're printouts of articles about Rowe I found online." Xander slid more papers toward the center of the table.

Wally picked one up. "Someone in one of these may have wanted her dead. Her... enthusiasm for storytelling has ruffled more than a few feathers."

"More like she plucked and roasted them." Tammy clamped her lips shut. Too late.

Mrs. Temperance wrapped her shawl tighter around her shoulders. "Didn't she have multiple arrests and warnings for harassment?"

Wally rubbed his chin. "Ms. Harvey wasn't afraid to cross the line if it meant getting the scoop."

Olivia held up an article. "It says here she hounded a grieving mother for an interview after her child went missing. The poor woman snapped and attacked Rowe in public."

Tammy's stomach knotted. This antagonist matched those she created for her books. Characters so determined that morality became optional. But this wasn't fiction. This was a real woman who had died a real death.

"Her tenacity made her as many enemies as headlines," said Mrs. T.

Tammy stroked Lockie's fur. In her novels, she'd narrow the suspect list to three compelling characters with interlocking motives. Actual life proved messier. "We need to figure out which of Rowe's targets made their move in Willowcroft."

A muscle twitched in Wally's jaw. "I've seen this before. Someone feels cornered or threatened, they lash out."

"Half the Midwest could have felt cornered," Xander said.

"Let's investigate the stories she's covered." Olivia organized the papers in front of her. "We'll need to split up and travel to other towns."

Tammy circled a name in one of the clippings. "We can start with the ones closest to home and work outward."

Olivia dropped her pen. "We've either got a massive suspect list or no direction at all."

Wally jotted a note in the margin of his sheet. "I'll reach out to detectives tied to these old cases and see if anyone remembers trouble."

Tammy bit the inside of her cheek. "Shouldn't we also consider that she was turning things around? Coming to a small town, focusing on historical mysteries instead of harassing people?"

Wally lifted an eyebrow. "People don't just wake up different. If she changed, I'd bet it wasn't by choice."

Tammy squared her shoulders. "If we paint Rowe as the villain from the start, we risk missing key evidence."

Olivia knocked her knuckles on the table. "You're right. We can't assume Rowe deserved this."

"I didn't say deserve." Wally clasped his hands on the table. "We must examine all potential motives. Professional and personal."

A small smile formed on Tammy's lips. She respected Wally's experience, even when their approaches differed. In her books, the detective and the sidekick had different methods that ultimately worked together.

Wally flipped through some of the articles. "Let's learn all we can about Rowe's history, good and bad. I'll focus on anyone with a grudge that might still be burning."

"We should also find out if Rowe received any threats before her murder," Olivia added.

Xander pushed his slipping glasses back in place. "And we can't forget about 'A' as our prime suspect."

Wally crossed his arms. "Do we have a complete list of her stories?"

"Working on it," Xander replied, typing on his laptop keyboard. "But considering she covered the entire Midwest, we're talking about a haystack's worth of needles."

"Then we start with the sharpest ones." Tammy squared her shoulders. The confidence usually reserved for her fictional detectives surged through her.

"We need to figure out what pushed the wrong person too far." Wally stood. "Motive means possibility. Possibility means suspect."

"Didn't she get run off the road after an exposé on a trucking company?" Olivia asked.

Tammy flipped through another article. "Yes. And shoved into a pool by an angry chef she accused of food poisoning."

"Or it could be someone local who feared what Rowe might uncover next," Xander said.

"Whichever it is, evidence is key," Wally stated. "And we need more of it."

Olivia cleared her throat. "Mr. Bonavy said Rowe was snooping around old family histories."

"We need to investigate both in town and out until we know for sure." Tammy arranged the articles in front of her like puzzle pieces. Was one of the names in front of her a killer? "Looks like we have our plans for tomorrow."

Xander closed his laptop with a slap. "Who's talking to whom?"

Chapter 13

Morning light crept around the edges of the bookstore's blinds. Olivia left them shut. Let the gawkers wonder. She taped a note to the door: "CLOSED DUE TO MURDER INVESTIGATION. DIRECT QUESTIONS ABOUT THE MUSEUM TO SHERIFF STANTON." The sheriff might curse her later, but she'd dealt with enough inquiries and had more important things to do.

She drove to Oaktown, where Ray glanced up from behind the bakery counter. Like all her regular customers, she knew him and his addiction for western novels well. He said the baking world was just another kind of frontier.

"Morning." Olivia pushed her glasses higher.

"What can I do for ya?" His smile faltered beneath a light dusting of white. "You riding in with trouble on your tail, or need a fix?"

"I was hoping to talk about Rowe Harvey." Olivia drummed her fingers on the counter's edge.

Ray smacked his palms together, sending a soft cloud into the air. "That woman rode into town like she was hunting outlaws. Wouldn't stop hounding me."

"Did she upset you?"

"Upset me?" He snorted. "She accused me of using 'questionable ingredients.' Said she'd title the episode *The Sourdough Scandal*. Real shoot-first-ask-questions-later kind of gal. Can you believe that?" Each exasperated gesture stirred the air, fine particles trailing like smoke.

"Did she threaten you?" Olivia studied the throbbing vein in his temple.

"Said she'd make sure I never sold another loaf in the Midwest." Red blotches spread across Ray's face.

"She said that?"

"And more. That woman made enemies like I make bread. Daily and with ease." The corners of his mouth twitched upward.

"Where were you on the night of Halloween?"

Ray flicked more flour across the counter. "I was here 'til after midnight. Halloween donuts are a thing now. People want them for breakfast the next day." He jabbed a thumb toward the racks behind him, where plump orange-glazed circles sat in neat rows. "Three of my staff stayed late decorating. The new kid left the oven on and almost burned the place down. Ask anyone. There was smoke, alarms, the entire block came out to watch us flail around with a fire extinguisher."

"That's... actually a solid alibi." Olivia's pen froze mid-note.

"Couldn't kill someone if I wanted to." He displayed his hands covered in blue plasters. "Each one of these marks a time I fainted dead away. Can't even handle the sight of my own papercuts without hittin' the floor. Pretty sure everyone in town has seen me go down at least once."

She jotted down his statement and paid for a Halloween donut. As she pushed the door, Ray called out, "Let me know when you catch the real jerk, will ya?"

She raised the bag in acknowledgment.

"I want to shake their hand. Might even name a loaf after them."

Olivia bolted through the door before he incriminated himself further. Hopefully, the others had rustled up something more substantial than a sugar-glazed alibi.

Chapter 14

"Let's grab snacks for the road." Tammy steered in the direction of the square. "Plus, I want to check out the latest tenant at Pippa's Pop-Ins."

She eased the car toward the curb. "These short-term rentals bring things to our little town we'd never see otherwise."

Lockie stared straight ahead, his whiskers rigid with focus.

"Less risky for everyone involved." Tammy's lips curved upward. "Remember the ice cream shop at the end of summer?"

Lockie's pink tongue darted across his mouth.

"I ate so much I swore off dairy for a month."

A sign proclaiming "Herbalist" hung above Pippa's storefront. Tammy parked, unbuckled her seatbelt, and hopped out. Lockie squirmed in her arms, then dropped to the sidewalk with a heavy thud, landing squarely on all fours. His ears pivoted like radar dishes.

A woman in a sunflower-patterned apron emerged from the store clutching a bulging wicker basket. Lockie froze. His pupils expanded to black pools. A strange, guttural sound rumbled from deep in his throat before he sprang forward with a piercing yowl.

Tammy lurched after him.

Lockie rubbed his cheeks against the woven basket, inhaling deeply.

"Is your cat having some kind of episode?" The woman clutched her belongings tighter.

Tammy gave her a level look. "He only acts this way when people are hiding something suspicious."

"How dare you!" The woman's face flushed crimson.

With a huff, the woman revealed a colorful array of dried herbs. Their pungent aroma hung heavy around them.

Lockie collapsed onto the pavement, his body vibrating with purrs so intense his whiskers trembled.

"Lucky for him he's cute." The woman's eyes narrowed.

"So much for his detective skills." Tammy sighed.

Lockie sprawled on his side, one paw waving lazily midair, eyes half-closed in apparent bliss.

"Is he... intoxicated?" Tammy crouched next to him.

"I assure you everything here is perfectly legal," the woman said.

The door to the shop tinkled as a tall man in a green apron stepped out. "Can I help with anything?"

Tammy pointed to Lockie, who now purred like a miniature motor, eyes glazed, paws batting at invisible objects. "Something in that basket turned my cat into... this."

"That's the valerian." The herbalist knelt beside Lockie. "Hits harder than catnip for some."

Tammy struggled to connect the polite-sounding herb with her blissed-out cat. "An herb does this?"

"My neighbor's tabby broke into my greenhouse just to roll in it." He stroked Lockie's fur. "We all have our weaknesses."

"Not Lockie." Tammy scooped up her limp cat. "I need him sharp for an interview with a suspect, not high as a kite."

"The effects only last ten to fifteen minutes."

"Let's hope so." Tammy tucked Lockie under her arm like a furry football. "Come on, party animal. We're off to Ann Arbor."

"That reporter ruined my family." The man across from Tammy crushed his work-worn hands into fists. "And now you think I killed her?"

Lockie's tail twitched against the floor. The cat never missed a lie.

"Let's start with facts, Mr. Garrett." She clicked her pen. "Rowe Harvey did a podcast about your family last year."

"A hatchet job." Garrett's knuckles whitened. "She dredged up my brother's arrest from twenty years back. The charges were dropped. It should've stayed buried. Then she made it everyone's business."

"So you confronted her about it?" Tammy kept her voice neutral.

"Damn right I did." Garrett slammed a palm on the table. "Told her she'd crossed a line."

Lockie's ears flattened. His tail flicked faster.

"But murder?" He shook his head. The words came softer now. "That's not me."

Garrett's fingers tapped the table once. Twice. Then curled into fists again. He lowered them to his lap and squeezed them together, veins straining beneath the skin.

"Can't say I shed tears over her death," he added.

"Anyone else hold a grudge strong enough to silence her permanently?" Tammy pressed.

Garrett eyed her cat. "Listen, Miss..."

"Rumbelow."

"Miss Rumbelow, folks in these parts don't appreciate strangers stirring up old ghosts." He adjusted his seat with a faint creak. "Rowe went rattling cages that were locked for a reason."

"Any names?"

He ran a finger along the edge of the table. "Check with the... Clark family." His gaze flicked away, then back again. Shoulders easing, he added, "Yeah, write that down."

The tightness in his jaw lingered.

Tammy scribbled 'Clarks' in her notebook. "Where were you on Halloween?"

Garrett sniffed and jabbed a thumb toward Lockie. "Your cat hasn't blinked once."

"Your alibi, Mr. Garrett."

"Working the chili stand in the Willowcroft town square until late. Got proof right here." He thrust his phone across the table, thick fingers smudging the cracked screen.

Lockie rose from his spot and brushed his nose against the edge of the device before backing away.

The photos told Garrett's story. They showed him in a gaudy orange apron, stirring a cauldron of beans at 6:30 p.m.; posing with costumed children; mock-wrestling everyone from the mayor to a pirate to Councilman Dean, a ladle masquerading as a broomstick; grinning alongside what appeared to be every resident of the town. The final image was timestamped 10:01 p.m.

"Didn't finish cleanup until 1 a.m." He crossed his arms. "The whole of Greater Willowcroft saw me serving the hottest chili in six counties."

He inspected his hands. "I've never cooked so much in one day before. My hands still have chili on them."

Tammy jotted notes. A lot of chili. A lot of time accounted for. She accepted the digital evidence. *But.*

"How does someone from Ann Arbor end up making chili in Willowcroft?"

"My old college roommate lives there. He loves my chili and asked if I wanted to make some extra money over the holiday."

She tucked away her notepad. Lockie sniffed at the man's pant leg. He lingered a few beats, then slunk to the door, tail low.

"Your cat..." Garrett pointed. "He stared at me the entire time."

"He knows truth from lies," she said as they stepped outside.

In the car, Lockie pounced onto the dashboard and pressed his nose against the vent.

"Fine, I'll turn the heat on for the drive home." Tammy started the engine. "Coming in person was risky. What if he had been the killer?"

The cat settled into the passenger seat, eyes half-lidded, face tilted into the flow of air.

"You'd warn me if I was in danger, right?" Tammy asked.

Lockie just purred, basking in the warm blast from the vent.

Chapter 15

Facts kept Wally sane throughout his career, but this case demanded he confront the messier world of motives and the murky waters of human emotion.

He tugged his coat into place and hammered a fist against the weathered door of a modest two-story house in Grand Rapids. Flakes of paint drifted to the concrete step below. The neighborhood stretched quiet and still.

The door opened. A man stood in the frame, deep creases across his brow, lines etched from nose to chin. David Keaton—victim of a podcast that had torn his life apart.

Wally flashed his ID. "I'm Mr. Wallace. Most people call me Wally. I'm investigating Rowe Harvey's death."

The man's facial muscles tightened. "Come in." He pivoted away, leaving Wally to follow.

The living room smelled of instant brew and disuse. Wally settled into a sagging armchair while Keaton dropped onto the couch. A coffee table with circular stains separated them. No photos adorned the walls. No plants softened the corners. The place of a man who'd lost more than his reputation.

"What can you tell me about your relationship with Ms. Harvey?" Wally planted his elbows on his knees and clasped his hands.

Keaton's fingers dug into the cushion beneath him. "Relationship? That woman ruined my life. Her podcast accused me of embezzling from the community center. Twenty years in this town, and overnight I became a thief." He jabbed a finger toward the window. "My kids can't even walk to school without hearing whispers. No one will give me a job."

"And it wasn't true?"

"The bookkeeping error had nothing to do with me. She never bothered to verify her 'sources' before broadcasting it to the world." Keaton's voice cracked. "You know what it's like to have strangers stare at you in the grocery store?"

The man carried enough anger to fill Boston Harbor. Wally shifted in his chair. "Did you confront her?"

"You bet I did!" Keaton sprang to his feet. "Wouldn't you? I told her she'd pay for the lies. I told her—" He stopped, nostrils flaring.

"You told her what?"

He sank back down. "I said she'd regret it. End of story."

"The restraining order suggests otherwise." Wally kept his tone neutral, a technique he'd perfected in interrogation rooms across Massachusetts.

"I went to her house. Raised my voice." Keaton's shoulders hunched. "But kill her? I couldn't. I wouldn't."

Wally tapped his fingers against his knee. "Anyone else who might've taken their grievances further?"

"Everyone hated her. Take your pick."

"Names would help."

"That's your job to figure out." His eyes narrowed. "Whoever silenced her... they ended my nightmare too."

"Let's keep sentiments like that to ourselves."

"Are we done?" Keaton's gaze fixed somewhere in the distance.

"Where were you Halloween night?" Wally studied the man's face, scanning for the micro-expressions that often betrayed liars.

"At Jim's Bar. Sat right at the counter from seven till closing." Keaton crossed his arms. "Jimmy poured every drink. He'll vouch for me."

Wally jotted the information in his notepad. "I'll be speaking with this bartender."

"You do that. Now get out and don't come back without a warrant."

Wally did check it out. Before he left Grand Rapids, he stopped by Jim's Bar and spoke to the owner himself, who confirmed Keaton had been there all evening, front and center. Rowe was last seen alive at seven. The timeline cleared Keaton.

Chapter 16

The team decided it was safest for Hazel to skip solo interviews, so she stayed home and baked scones to help clear her head. A chime rang through the kitchen as she measured the ingredients. She wiped flour-dusted hands on her apron and tapped her phone awake. The Knotty but Nice group chat had exploded with messages.

Della Mae: Just spoke to Georgina at the inn! She said Rowe stayed there a month or so ago.

Betty: SHE'S BEEN HERE BEFORE???

Beatrice: Who's Rowe?

Marjorie: The woman from the museum, Bea. Honestly.

Betty: You know what's still funny? George and Georgina running the inn. It's like a tongue twister every time I say it. George and Georgina Gregson, innkeepers!

Marjorie: You don't choose who you love based on their name. Must we discuss this every single time they come up?

Betty: I think it's adorable. Imagine meeting someone with your name and falling in love! Like a storybook!

Beatrice: My neighbor once dated a man named Herb. She couldn't stand cooking after that.

Hazel smiled, mixing the flour and butter together before she replied.

Hazel: That's helpful, Dell. I had assumed this was Rowe's first time in Willowcroft. Knowing she's been before changes things.

Betty: Is it suspicious? It *feels* suspicious. Like she was snooping.

Marjorie: Or, you know, a weekend getaway.

Beatrice: Why did she come the first time? Did Georgina say?

Della Mae: Just that she wasn't happy that Rowe was returning.

Betty: Ohhhh, I wonder why?

Hazel dusted her hands clean.

Hazel: I'm making scones. Might stop by the inn later with a warm batch. Georgina talks more with a mouthful of jam and cream.

Betty: BRILLIANT. The Scone Strategy. We should trademark that!

Marjorie: It's hardly espionage, Betty. It's baking.

Beatrice: What kind of scones?

Hazel: Classic this time. I've got raspberry jam that needs using.

Della Mae: Casually mention her guests are now part of a senior citizen spy ring.

Betty: "Scone and Surveillance" is our next club name!!!

Marjorie: I'm muting this conversation now.

Marjorie has left the chat.

Betty: Oh no, she's gone again. Someone bring her back with logic or lemon curd.

Hazel: I'll save her a scone. That usually works.

Hazel set the phone aside, smiling as she rolled out the dough. A little gossip, a little butter—both brought results in Willowcroft.

Hazel removed the scones from the oven. Perfect golden tops. She tucked them into a basket, swaddling them in a checkered cloth to keep them warm.

"Right then, time to get a wriggle on." She buttoned her coat over a teal shawl.

The brisk fall air nipped at her cheeks as she strolled toward the Willowcroft Inn a block past the opposite side of the square. Every third cobblestone wobbled, a mental map she'd created over a lifetime in town.

Georgina stood behind the reception desk, wearing her usual pinched expression. But as the scent of fresh-baked goods drifted through the doorway, her features softened.

"Aren't you a dear. What's the occasion?" The innkeeper accepted the offering with a quick glance inside.

"Oh, just a little thank you for all you do for our town." Hazel flashed her warmest smile, the one she'd perfected for parents' evenings at school. "I have a question, if you have a moment. I heard from a friend that a certain... unsavory character has been staying here recently."

Georgina's face darkened. "Ah, you must mean Ms. Harvey. I'll make tea to go with the scones."

The instant Georgina disappeared with the basket, Hazel sprang into action. The guest log lay open on the counter, ink still wet on the latest entry. This was her chance!

Forty years of teaching had gifted her with the ability to read text at any angle. All those students and their secret notes had been training in disguise. The handwriting in the inn's book might as well have been printed in large type.

Rowe Harvey. There it was, scrawled in hasty, bold letters. Hazel scanned the entries surrounding it, her eyes fixing on the date of the murder. She whipped out her notepad and scribbled. She turned back the pages to find the previous visit as the kettle whistled.

The pad vanished into her pocket as Georgina returned, balancing a tea tray and leading Hazel into the lounge area.

"Reporter or something," Georgina said, arranging cups on the small table as if their conversation had never paused. "I prefer not to speak ill of the dead, but she was nothing but trouble during her stays."

Stays? The intel was correct. "How so?"

"She demanded things at all hours." She poured the tea. "And so rude and abrasive with my other guests and staff too. I couldn't wait for her to check out."

"Goodness gracious." Hazel sipped her tea.

Georgina sighed. "I was quite shocked when she had the nerve to return. Thankfully it was a shorter visit before, well, you know."

"Who knows what state she's left the room in. The sheriff hasn't let me in there to clean yet. After her first stay, it took me an entire afternoon to set things right again."

"Did she leave anything behind?" Hazel kept her tone casual.

"Magazines strewn around the room. The pages were all cut up, like some sort of project."

"Did you keep them?"

"Of course." She pushed back from the table. "I keep everything left behind for three months in case people call asking after them. It's not my place to say what is or isn't important to someone."

"Did you give them to the sheriff?"

"In the shock, I clear forgot about them until you asked me just now."

"Do you think I could have them?"

Georgina strode to a cupboard in the corner and retrieved a cardboard box. She placed it in Hazel's waiting hands.

Hazel flipped through the mangled magazines, noting the precise cuts and missing letters. "This is very helpful."

Hazel left the inn with her basket much heavier than when she arrived. The scraps of paper inside might hold clues to what Rowe Harvey was doing in Willowcroft.

Chapter 17

Olivia sat upright, the stiff wooden chair pressing into her back as she ignored the cold piece of pizza cooling beside her notebook. Notes and half-formed theories cluttered the table, while Wally stood in front of the murder board, arms folded. The whole thing was a tangle of arrows, headlines, and question marks.

"Let's examine the facts," he said.

The room quieted. Olivia reached for a pen with renewed focus. Across from her, Tammy clicked her pen in a sharp, deliberate rhythm. Mrs. Temperance paused mid-stitch.

"Rowe was last seen at seven by George at the inn, presumably on her way to the museum where she was killed."

He stepped back from the board, giving the timeline a once-over. "Three alibis from the podcast-related suspects. Fire extinguishers, chili, and beer place them elsewhere after seven."

Tammy leaned in, pen poised. "What else do we know about Rowe's movements?"

Wally glanced at Mrs. T, who said, "She was sighted in the square at six thirty."

"Then returned to the inn," Wally added. "George said she ordered pizza, paid for it, and left in a hurry before it even arrived. She was dead within the hour."

Olivia shifted in her seat. What made her leave with such urgency?

Xander spun his laptop toward them. "Rowe deleted emails from the Michaels and Grey families. One told her to back off. The other seemed willing to talk."

Olivia let out a low groan. "Not them again. They always end up as red herrings."

"Until they don't," Mrs. T said, her needles still for once.

"And the first message from 'A' came soon after the tunnel news broke this summer," Xander added.

There's no way that's a coincidence with Rowe's instincts.

"She was in town about a month ago," Mrs. T said. "Left a pile of magazines at the inn. Georgina passed them on to me. None of the entries I saw in the register have helped so far."

Olivia's attention flicked back to the board as Wally stepped up again. He picked up a marker, underlining names. "Time to shift back to local and bootlegging leads. The Michaels, the Greys, and the Walshes."

"Clark Michaels," Tammy said. "Maybe that's who Garrett meant when he said 'the Clarks'..."

"Could be," Wally said.

"Although," she added, "the way he said it almost sounded like he was trying to redirect."

"Either way, we follow that thread," said Wally. "Dig into the tunnel's history and the people who used it—or wanted it buried."

"I'll keep working through Rowe's deleted emails," Xander said, fingers already flying across his keyboard. "If I can find what she was about to expose, we'll know who had the most to lose."

Lockie stirred near the wall, his tail thumping once on the floor before he burrowed deeper into the blanket pile.

Olivia recalled the book she'd ordered too late to be of use during their previous investigation.

She fetched the step ladder and climbed to the top shelf of the kitchenette.

Olivia balanced precariously as she peered into the cabinet. "It has to be here somewhere."

Fingers stretched toward the far edge and brushed something solid. "Aha!"

She tugged the hardcover free: *Bootleggers and Bandits: The Michaels Family in Prohibition Michigan*. It arrived after they'd branded the families as red herrings. Maybe this time it would fill in the gaps.

Tucking it under one arm, Olivia hopped down and adjusted her cardigan.

Wally appeared poised to catch her should she fall. Mrs. T sat in the comfortable armchair knitting. Xander paid no attention, while Tammy eyed what Olivia was doing.

Olivia slid the book onto the table. "This might help us understand the connection between the Michaels, Grey, and Walsh families."

Wally straightened.

Olivia tapped the book's cover. "This arrived after we wrapped up the bank heist. I skimmed it, then placed it somewhere safe."

"And safe means a cupboard near the cereal?" asked Tammy.

Four pairs of eyes stared at her. Even Lockie paused his grooming to fix her with a judgmental squint.

"Any particular reason you stored valuable research material next to breakfast?" Wally asked.

Olivia sat and sipped her coffee, buying time. "I put it there after reading an interesting passage about how the families hid their most important documents in unusual places—kitchen canisters, false-bottomed drawers, hollowed-out books. I suppose I got a bit... inspired."

"You hid a book about hiding things by hiding it yourself?" Tammy asked, a smile playing on her lips.

"It marinated better that way," Olivia said. "Ideas need to steep sometimes. And I didn't want to misplace it."

Mrs. T sniffed. "What does it say?"

Olivia opened to a page she'd dog-eared. "According to this, all three families collaborated on the bootlegging front but suggests there was a bigger player running the enterprise."

Olivia turned to a photograph of three men standing side by side. "Clark Michaels, Samuel Grey, and Victor Walsh. It's the same one we got from Peter Walsh when looking for the missing money, but the caption says this was taken before a feud over bank heist rumors tore the families apart."

"We know none of them had anything to do with the robbery," said Tammy.

"But we never considered a higher power," said Wally.

"And Rowe figured out who it was?" asked Xander.

Lockie leaped onto the table, sniffing at the book before settling beside it, his tail flicking against the pages.

"They may not be red herrings this time," Olivia said. "I'll go through it line by line, and I'll expand their family trees to see if there's a connection we missed."

Lockie stretched, jumped down, and sauntered toward the storage room.

"Where's he going?" Wally asked.

Olivia smiled. "Probably checking if I've hidden any other books, or food, in strange places. Cats appreciate a good mystery."

Wally gathered his notes. "Let's reconvene in the morning. We'll review any updates and then decide our next move."

Lockie returned and launched himself onto the table. As Olivia gently nudged him aside, the team packed up.

At least I know what I'm doing tomorrow.

Chapter 18

Wally sipped his lukewarm coffee, the bookstore's morning quiet broken only by the soft click of Tammy's pen, the rustle of Olivia turning a page in her bootlegging book, and the rhythm of Mrs. Temperance's knitting needles creating something that looked like it might strangle anyone who wore it.

Lockie dozed beside the heater like he hadn't a care in the world. Wally envied him.

Xander burst through the disguised door, breathless, his backpack hanging half-zipped from one shoulder.

"You're meant to be at school," Mrs. T said.

Xander waved her off. "I've got something. I think I found our 'A.'"

Wally lowered his mug. "Talk."

"Rowe was investigating the Adams family of Detroit."

A warning siren rang in Wally's mind. He knew that name. Everyone in law enforcement did. That family had a reputation stretching decades. They'd sidestepped charges again and again, their money buying silence and fear in equal measure.

"They're famously wealthy," Xander said, flipping open his laptop, "and have long been rumored to have built their fortune during Prohibition."

Wally's posture stiffened. "Go on."

"Rowe accused Emerson Adams of money laundering and mob connections. She even showed up at his estate. He sent his sons to chase her off."

Tammy stared at him. "And this is all in the emails?"

"No, a podcast episode from a few weeks back."

Wally tapped a finger against the tabletop. "If we dig deeper into this angle, we have to do so carefully."

"Samuel Grey married into an Adams family," Olivia said as she flipped through folders. "Could it be the same family?"

"You do your genealogy thing and tell us," Wally said to Olivia before turning to Xander. "I want to hear what Rowe had to say about them."

Xander nodded. "I've got it queued."

Wally crossed his arms. "Let's see if I'm driving to Detroit today."

[Background music playing]

"Welcome back to another thrilling episode of 'True Crime Chronicles.' I'm your host, Rowe Harvey, here to take you on a journey into the murky world of crime, cash flow, and conspiracies. In today's episode, we delve deep into the secrets of one notorious Detroit family."

[Music fades out]

"Now, you may think you know everything about the Adams family. The glamorous parties, the influential connections, the lavish lifestyle. But the truth behind their rise is more sinister than you could ever imagine.

"Let's turn back the clock to the Prohibition era, a time when illegal alcohol flowed through secret channels into speakeasies. The Adamses didn't just profit from this era, they dominated it, becoming central figures in Michigan's shadow economy.

"Legends speak of navigating the moonlit back roads of Michigan, trading barrels of moonshine for wads of cash. Those early deals weren't just profitable; they laid the foundation for a dynasty built on secrecy and control.

"But bootlegging was only the beginning. The family expanded into underground gambling dens where the elite could indulge far from prying eyes. These operations offered both strategic and financial gains. By catering to the powerful, the Adamses secured protection and influence that money alone couldn't buy.

"How did they make their wealth appear clean? Through a carefully constructed façade. Florists, car dealerships, shipping companies, and more masqueraded as fronts to funnel dirty money into the mainstream economy. On paper, they were model entrepreneurs.

"But the burning question remains: How did the Adams family remain uncaught and out of jail? Some believe it was their close ties to certain members of law enforcement and politicians. A web of corruption and cover-ups protected their criminal empire from scrutiny.

"As time passed, their influence evolved. From liquor and gambling, they ventured into narcotics and political manipulation. What began as a family business became a sophisticated empire of control and deception.

"Despite the rumors, concrete evidence has always been scarce. Those who dared to dig too deep often faced dire consequences. I myself had a run-in with them."

[Transition sound effect]

"Sadly, dear listeners, our time together has come to an end. But remember, even the most polished families can conceal darkness beneath the shine. The Adams legacy may no longer dominate headlines, but their legacy persists, forever etched into the dark annals of history."

[Background music fades in]

"That's all for today's episode of True Crime Chronicles. Thank you for joining me in this journey through the murky depths of the Adams Family's history. There's more to come on this story. I've only just begun my investigation—and let's just say, sometimes the smallest scraps reveal the biggest truths.

"Until next time, stay safe, and keep your eyes open. Who knows what secrets the people around you might be hiding?

[Music fades out]

"She wasn't pulling any punches, was she?" Olivia said.

Wally shook his head, his expression grim. "No wonder they came after her. These are dangerous allegations."

"Do you really think the Adams family could be involved in her murder?" Tammy asked.

"It's a possibility," Wally said. "Especially if there's a connection here through the Greys."

Wally stood, already reaching for his jacket. "I'm going to Detroit. If Emerson Adams, the current patriarch, knows something, I plan to find out what."

"Alone?" Tammy asked.

Mrs. Temperance folded her knitting. "Be careful. Men like that don't appreciate questions."

Wally met her gaze. He'd dealt with types like Emerson Adams before. Smooth talkers who wrapped their threats in silk ties and let money do the talking. They didn't scare him. Not anymore.

He crossed the room in three strides, each step firm with purpose. Lockie padded after him, biting at his pant leg like a deputy refusing to be left behind.

Wally paused to glance down. "You stay here and protect the team."

Chapter 19

With Wally off to Detroit, Xander packed off back to school, Olivia buried in genealogy records, and Tammy going into the Prohibition book, Hazel set off on her own to Serenity Gardens nursing home to visit Eleanor Bennett. She was the only one left in town who had met some of the players the team was investigating.

Eleanor had played a key role in unraveling what happened in Willowcroft during the fifties with the murder of Mary Collins committed by her brother Max Cross, the bank heist, and the long-lost tunnels. Maybe she could shed light on this mystery too.

"Good morning, Mrs. Temperance," chirped nurse Emma, sporting scrubs depicting black cats. The nurse was as famous for her unique work attire as Hazel was for her colorful shawls.

"Morning, dear."

Hazel clutched an old photograph to her chest as she navigated the hall with purpose, her sensible shoes making a soft patter on the floor. The photo, yellowed with age, depicted Victor Walsh, Samuel Grey, and Clark Michaels in their heyday of the 1950s. It was their parents' and grandparents' generations involved in Prohibition. But they were in their twenties when the bank heist took place, which may have caused a feud among the families.

She opened the door and stepped inside, finding Eleanor seated by the window. The sun cast a warm glow on her short, white hair, illuminating her delicate features. Despite being of fragile frame, there was a strength and resilience in Eleanor that Hazel had always admired.

"What brings you here today with such a storm in your eyes?" the older woman asked.

"You always see right through me."

Hazel approached and extended the photograph toward her. "I need your eagle eye for something. Does this picture stir anything in your vault of secrets?"

The woman examined the image. Her expression tightened as she studied the faces captured within it. Her fingers trembled as they brushed the surface. For a moment, confusion flickered; then her eyes brightened, and she spoke.

"Goodness, where did you dig up this old fossil?" Eleanor's tone was playful, but the intensity in her gaze hadn't faded.

"Found it among the papers given to us by Peter Walsh, Victor Walsh's son." Hazel lowered her voice to a conspiratorial whisper. "What do you remember about these three? They were thick as thieves back in the day, weren't they?"

Eleanor's lips quirked into a smile, the corners of her eyes crinkling. "Oh, indeed they were. The Walshes, the Greys, the Michaels... they were as close as kin when I was a sprout. But then..." A shadow crossed her features.

"Then the feud?" Hazel perched on the edge of her chair. "You think it happened after the bank heist? Could it be they turned on each other, each pointing fingers?"

Eleanor paused, her gaze distant as she considered the question. "Rumors swirled around town, whisperings about how each family might have been involved in the robbery, but I assumed it was my brother, so I didn't pay much attention."

"They would have known about the tunnel system under Willowcroft from their grandparents' bootlegging days. It wouldn't take much to believe one thought another had used it to pull it off."

"Perhaps..." Eleanor murmured. "It's all so tangled, like yarn after a kitten's had its way. Old suspicions, doubts. Hard to sort truth from gossip."

"But you have the sharpest claws for this task."

Eleanor gave a small nod. "The feud created deep bitterness and distrust. They couldn't work together anymore. It's a shame. These three were like brothers."

"By the way, you seem to be doing well. Your memory is sharp, and you're as bright as ever." Hazel smiled warmly at her friend. "It's heartening to see you so engaged, considering..."

"Considering what everyone assumes about me?" Eleanor said with a wry head tilt. The frailness of her frame belied the sharpness still alive behind the pale curtain of her eyes.

"Exactly. The whispers of dementia are often louder than the truth, but you've been defying expectations."

Eleanor sighed, a fragile sound that filled the room with vulnerability. "Oh, Hazel, there are days when I let those murmurs win."

"Whatever do you mean?" Hazel's nurturing nature now intermingled with curiosity.

"Can you keep a secret?" Eleanor asked with a twinkle of mischief in her eye. "Sometimes it's easier to pretend. I fake forgetfulness here and there."

Hazel's eyes widened in surprise. Then she shook her head. "You rascal! Don't you worry, dear, your confidence is safe with me."

The two older women giggled like school children.

"We all find ways to cope," said Hazel. "With your brother's history, of course they believe you. Just promise you won't overdo it, all right? You're too valuable to lose."

"I only do it when necessary." Eleanor's shoulders lifted in a tiny shrug. "If I don't want to attend another tedious activity or if someone becomes too inquisitive... A touch of confusion, a misplaced word, and they leave me be."

"I must say, your ingenuity never ceases to amaze me."

"Thank you, Hazel." Eleanor's expression softened. "It's comforting to have a confidante who understands the game."

"Speaking of games, Wally tells me he's worked out a way to get you into the museum once it's allowed to open."

"How marvelous!" Eleanor clasped her hands together. "It's been a childhood dream of mine to explore those old passageways."

"Consider it a promise from the team."

"Why are you still digging into these families? I thought everything was solved."

"We're investigating the recent death of a podcaster in the tunnels."

"How does that relate to the old families?"

"We think Ms. Harvey discovered a link between the nefarious Adams family in Detroit and Willowcroft during Prohibition."

"A Charlotte Adams married one of the boys, didn't she? Is there a connection?"

"Good memory. Olivia's working on it as we speak. Is there anything you think might be helpful?"

"Charlotte wasn't from town, but she was a regular visitor, I know that."

"Every detail counts."

"You've stumbled into another adventure. You really do lead an exciting life, Hazel."

"It keeps me young, I can tell you. I'll update you as we go. You're an essential part of our team."

Eleanor's eyes shone with gratitude. "I can't wait."

With a final affectionate squeeze of Eleanor's hand, Hazel rose. "Take care, dear. I'll be back with more updates and scones."

Chapter 20

Wally flashed his old detective credentials at the security camera. A sheriff's shield from Willowcroft wouldn't get him far in Detroit, but both Boston and HOMICIDE commanded respect. Most folks skimmed past the *retired* etched below. The oldest trick still worked.

The iron gates towering over him creaked apart. He followed the winding path to the Adams mansion, a monument of glass and stone dominating the landscape.

The front door opened before Wally reached the first step. A butler stood waiting, expressionless but efficient, and took his coat.

"Mr. Adams will see you now," he said, acknowledging authority without conceding ground.

"Lead the way."

They moved through vast rooms filled with museum-quality art and furniture worth more than Wally's house. Their footsteps rang against marble as they passed a grand piano and a painting of hunters on horseback. The butler stopped at heavy oak doors and pushed them to reveal a room arranged like a ship's bridge. A commanding chair sat behind an imposing slab of mahogany.

"Mr. Adams, your appointment has arrived."

Emerson Adams Jr. occupied the space like a monarch. Broad-shouldered and immovable, he loomed behind the desk, every item arranged with military precision. Close-cropped gray hair matched the cold glint in his eyes. His Italian suit probably cost more than Wally's monthly pension, yet it fit like a second skin.

"Detective Wallace," Adams said, his voice smooth as polished steel. "Quite the journey from Boston."

Wally dropped into an overstuffed leather chair across from him without invitation. "I've always liked to travel."

Adams settled back as if he owned every conversation in the room. He pressed his fingertips together. "I trust you'll be discreet?"

Wally locked eyes with him. "I trust I'll get the facts."

Adams dipped his chin. "What do you want to know?"

The butler materialized with a silver tray bearing delicate china that trembled with each step. Wally accepted one. His host's hand remained as steady as stone.

Steam curled from the rim. "I need to ask about Rowe Harvey." Wally focused on Adams' face.

Adams blinked twice. His fingers tapped once against his cup before freezing. The name alone triggered something. His eyes narrowed, an infinitesimal constriction Wally might have missed if he hadn't spent years observing guilty men.

Adams set his drink down. "I already told the police everything I know about that woman."

"Humor me." He rested his arms on the chair. "When did Rowe Harvey first contact you?"

Adams's back went rigid. "About three months ago. She left threatening messages, claiming she had evidence I laundered money. Wanted an interview."

"I assume you declined?"

"Of course! Pure slander." Adams slammed his fist on the desk, rattling the surface. "She shouted accusations through my intercom one night. I sent my boys to remove her."

"Your sons roughed her up, correct?"

Adams's jaw locked. "They encouraged her swift departure. I don't tolerate trespassing and defamation."

Wally set down his cup and sat back, indicating it was time for real answers.

"We have excellent security," Adams added after a calculated pause.

"I saw that."

The corner of Adams's mouth twitched, unusual for a man who prided himself on being unreadable.

"What can you tell me about her murder in Willowcroft?" Wally kept his tone casual. "Strange location for it."

Adams froze. Color drained from his face, and his pupils contracted to pinpoints. "Willow...croft?" He swallowed hard, the Adam's apple bobbing beneath the silk tie. "I wasn't aware..." The words caught, and his voice cracked. Either genuine shock or an Academy Award performance. A temple vein pulsed.

"But the name rings familiar, doesn't it?" Wally inched forward. Adams had reacted to the town name. Something significant lurked there. Wally's instincts screamed at him not to let it go.

"Tell me about the break-in." Wally had done his homework.

Adams blinked. "Break-in?"

"A few weeks back. Your housekeeper called the police. Spotted a figure near the bins and heard noises."

Adams waved a dismissive hand. "That woman's nerves are strung tighter than a Steinway. Probably a raccoon. Detroit teems with them."

"It was logged as a robbery."

Adams exhaled sharply. "They found nothing. No damage. Nothing taken."

"That raises questions." Wally sipped his coffee, allowing silence to build pressure. "An intruder breaches your security and takes nothing? Doesn't make sense."

Adams lifted one shoulder. "Vandals. Protesters. Some people resent success."

"Success rarely motivates people who steal nothing."

Adams's lips thinned into a smile, acknowledging Wally's point without verbal concession. "Perhaps they were interrupted."

"Or perhaps they sought something only you know is missing."

Adams's expression hardened. He pushed back his chair and rose. "I'm done being interrogated by *retired* detectives."

The guard hadn't missed it. Why agree to see him? Curiosity? Guilt? Something else?

"You seem nervous, Mr. Adams."

"We're done here." Adams strode to the door, each step a dismissal. "Leave my property at once."

Wally held his gaze, detecting fear beneath the bluster. He stood with a brief gesture. "Of course. Thank you for your time." As he walked out, he spotted Adams's hands. They trembled.

He made his way through the mansion with unhurried confidence. The butler appeared and handed him his coat.

Wally drove through the exit gates, replaying the conversation. "Willowcroft" had shattered Adams's composure more than Rowe Harvey's name. Adams knew the town and feared it.

Time to dig into the family's roots.

Chapter 21

Lockie sprang onto the table. The others jerked back in surprise, but Wally stayed still.

He stood, scraping his chair back. "It was Rowe. That robbery at the Adams estate where nothing was taken? She did it."

Tammy's hand stilled, her pen hovering over the page. "But nothing was stolen, right? That's what the report said, and Emerson confirmed that."

"Nothing obvious." Wally rubbed his thumb across his knuckles. "Doesn't mean it was fruitless."

Mrs. Temperance laid her knitting on her lap. "You think she traveled to Detroit to stage a break-in?"

"She staged nothing." Wally paced as he spoke. "The housekeeper spotted someone near the bins, panicked, and called the cops. When they arrived, the intruder had vanished. No forced entry. Nothing listed as missing."

Xander looked up from his laptop, the screen's glow catching on his lenses. "So what... Rowe went dumpster diving?"

"People toss out their secrets without a second thought." Wally halted at the backdoor window. "Notes, drafts, bills, envelopes with handwritten traces. I solved a case once when a suspect threw away a receipt with his hotel alias scrawled on the back."

Olivia seized her mug with both hands. "And with the correct timing, she could find something important that nobody bothered to destroy."

"Right on target." Wally turned to face the group. "Who keeps track of yesterday's trash? If she linked the Adams family to past crimes or current ones, their garbage became gold."

Tammy tapped her pen on a notepad. The fast, nervous clicks grated against Wally's focus. "Her words from the podcast make sense now," she said. "'The smallest scraps can reveal the biggest truths.'"

Mrs. T cut a thread with her tiny silver scissors. "Brilliant tactic. The mansion itself is too secure. But the bins? That's where protection fails."

Xander adjusted his glasses. "She didn't need to enter the house."

"She acquired her prize." Wally dropped back into his chair. "And whatever it was... it terrified Adams enough to erase her existence from his memory."

In the quiet that followed, even Lockie stopped his attack on the speaker cord.

Olivia slammed her mug onto the table. "So what did she uncover in the garbage that cost her life?"

Tammy closed her notebook with a snap. "And does it still exist somewhere, waiting for us?"

"I don't like this one bit," said Wally. "All of you, pack a bag. You're staying at mine tonight."

Lockie twitched an ear at the shift in the room's energy.

"Are we in danger?" Tammy asked.

"I'm not taking any chances," Wally replied, meeting each of their gazes with his own steely one. "Especially not after what happened to Rowe. Maybe I shouldn't have gone to the Adams house."

Wally glanced at his watch. "I'm going to check in with Stanton, see if they have unearthed anything we could use while you pack. I'll meet you back at mine a.s.a.p."

He grabbed his coat and headed out into the crisp November air, the leaves crunching underfoot as he made the short trek across the square to the sheriff's building.

The sheriff peered up from a cluttered desk, his face weary but attentive at Wally's entrance.

"Wallace, what brings you here?"

"Got any updates on the Harvey case?" Wally scanned the room for signs of progress.

"Actually, we do," Stanton said, pulling out an evidence bag containing several crumpled pieces of paper. "We found some threatening letters in Rowe Harvey's inn room. They're our main lead right now."

"Threats?" He inspected them through the plastic. Old-school cut-and-paste lettering.

"We're trying to figure out who sent them," Stanton confessed, running a hand over his stubbled chin. "She had enemies in every town she visited."

"Did you find any fingerprints?" Wally asked, his focus sharp as he watched Stanton's reaction.

"Only Rowe's."

"Interesting." He recalled Mrs. T's magazines. "There could be a reason for that."

Stanton gave a quizzical look.

"Have you investigated the Grey family yet? They've got some deep roots here, and there may be a connection to the Adams family out in Detroit. Ms. Harvey did a podcast about them."

Stanton's posture locked, tension radiating off him before he even spoke. "Organized crime Adams family? That's a serious accusation."

"Rumors are rumors until they're not," Wally replied with a slight shrug. "But it wouldn't hurt to check out all angles, right? Especially with Rowe poking into dark corners."

"True," Stanton conceded, jotting down a note. "I'll put them on the list."

"Good man," Wally said, clapping Stanton on the shoulder.

"By the way," Wally added nonchalantly, "the team's staying at mine for a while to be on the safe side."

"Is that so?" Stanton asked, his gaze sharpening.

"Keeping an extra eye on things, just in case."

"You've got good instincts. I'll make sure we maintain a heightened level of vigilance around town."

"Much appreciated."

"Take care. And keep me updated on any developments on your end."

"Will do," Wally assured him.

"Guys, I want to say thanks for agreeing to stay here with me," Wally began, his voice warm and sincere. "I know it might seem like an overreaction, but there's no harm in being cautious."

They reconvened under the glow of Wally's porch light. The night air carried a crispness hinting at the coming winter.

"Stick close, everyone." His protective instincts flared as dusk settled outside. "We don't know if the threat ended with Rowe, or if it's the beginning."

"Let's set up in the living room," Tammy said. "I want answers before we're the next ones making headlines."

"Rowe's investigation could have been what got her killed," Olivia chimed in. "But was it the Willowcroft angle, or something else?"

"Or someone else," said Mrs. T. "We've got the Michaels, Grey, and Walsh connections to consider."

"And the Adams family," said Wally.

Olivia displayed a family tree diagram. "The Adams family Samuel Grey married into is the same as the one in Detroit."

"Let's not forget about 'A,'" Xander interjected, his youthful eagerness to contribute overshadowed by the gravity of the situation. "Whoever that is, they knew Rowe would bite at the chance for a scoop."

They settled around Wally's kitchen table, which was strewn with documents. Lockie curled up on the windowsill, keeping watch with half-lidded eyes.

"Schoolwork first," Xander muttered to himself. "But how can equations compete with real-life crime-solving?"

"Algebra might help you solve a crime one day," said Mrs. T.

"Wally, have you ever used math to solve a crime?" asked Xander.

"Homework first," Wally replied. "But I need to tell you about the letters Stanton showed me. The words were cut from magazines to form a message: Talk or be talked about. I couldn't read the others."

"She received multiple threats?" asked Mrs. T.

"I'm not so sure," said Wally. "The only fingerprints on them were Rowe's."

"So the sender wore gloves. Everyone knows that thanks to movies and TV shows," said Olivia.

"Mrs. T, didn't you say you had magazines found in Rowe's room?" asked Wally.

"Yes. Are you saying Rowe made them herself?"

"She was spooking people into talking," Tammy concluded. "I don't like her tactics."

"But those ones didn't reach their target," said Xander.

"Could she have been giving the Adams family time to tell their own story before she did it for them?" suggested Tammy.

"They would benefit from her silence," said Wally.

"Or was she being set up?" Olivia's fingers tapped an uneven rhythm on her knee. "Framing her as the one sending threats?"

"If you wanted to discredit someone, making them appear unhinged is one way to do it," said Wally.

"Rowe's methods were... unorthodox," Tammy said. "But I can't say she didn't have guts."

"Unorthodox is putting it mildly," Wally grumbled. "She drove folks to paranoia."

"We're dealing with the aftermath of her actions," Tammy reminded the group. "We need to tread carefully. Did the sheriff say anything about the Greys?"

"I told him to add them to his list," Wally replied. "If Rowe was digging into old mob ties... she might have unearthed more than she bargained for."

"Old grudges can lead to new vendettas," Mrs. T said.

Wally rose to check the locks. "We've got a great deal to work through. Best get some rest while we can."

They filed into the bunk bedroom Wally had designed for his grand-children. Despite only knowing each other a few months, this wasn't their first time bunking together. Safety in numbers had quickly become their unspoken policy.

The two sets of bunk beds housed four of them while Wally took his own room down the hall. With the sheriff's building just three doors down, it was close enough for a quick response yet private enough for candid strategy sessions.

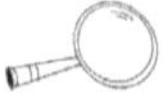

In the middle of the night, a knock on the door jolted the team awake. Wally cracked the door to find Stanton, concern etching deep lines into his face.

"Sorry to disturb," the sheriff apologized, "but you should know Miss Huddlestone's bookstore window was smashed in by a pumpkin and set off the alarms. We're looking into it, but I wanted to make sure everyone was okay."

"Thank you for checking on us," Olivia said, rubbing her eyes as she joined Wally at the door. "Is there anything we can do?"

"Right now, just stay here," Stanton instructed. "I'm leaving Brown behind to stand guard in case the perpetrator has any other plans for the night." As the sheriff prepared to leave, he offhandedly added, "Oh, by the way, you're all off the suspect list."

"That's one less thing to worry about," Wally said while closing the door.

"Who knew running a bookstore could be so dangerous?" Olivia sighed. "My insurance company is going to think I've taken up juggling hammers."

"Better than being the target of a hammer thrower," Mrs. T pointed out, earning a weary chuckle.

"Or a group of toddlers." The room erupted in laughter as they recalled the absurdity of the previous incident when toddler storytime resulted in a broken window.

"Maybe you should start selling books about self-defense alongside your mystery novels," Xander joked.

"Or window glazing for dummies," Mrs. T suggested.

"I told you booking Mike in advance was a good idea," said Olivia.

"I know what Olivia's going to be dreaming about," Xander said.

"But why my store?" Olivia asked, ignoring Xander.

Wally put a reassuring hand on her shoulder. "Maybe a member of the Adams family is sending a message."

"But how would they even know to associate me with your investigation in the first place?"

"They could have followed me after my visit, where I went straight to the bookstore to update you all. We may be under surveillance," Wally said. "It's important we stay prudent from here on out."

"Back to sleep, everyone," Mrs. T said.

"Sleep? With all this excitement?" Tammy said, though her words were betrayed by a yawn.

"Come on," Wally encouraged, a faint smile on his lips despite the circumstances. "We've got a crime to solve after dawn, and we need to be sharp."

They nestled back into their childish bunk beds. Deputy Brown outside provided a small cocoon of safety.

Chapter 22

Tammy paced the three steps to the window and back again. Her fingers twisted the pendant at her throat as she considered the implications of Wally's confrontation with the Adams family.

She paused at the coffee table, rearranged the scattered notes into neat piles, then disturbed them again. The curtains remained drawn despite the hours of daylight that had passed. Someone dangerous now had their sights set on her and her friends.

She joined Wally, who was scanning the quiet street for any suspicious activity. "Do you think they're watching us now?" she asked.

Wally put a reassuring hand on her shoulder. "Hard to say, but Brown is outside. He'll let us know if there's anything to worry about."

Tammy focused on the team huddled in Wally's lounge room.

Xander's dad, Park Ranger Dan, had picked up Xander and driven him to school. Mrs. T was making a fresh pot of coffee, and Olivia was focused on her genealogical databases.

Tammy tucked a strand of hair behind her ear. Who should they focus on? The Adams family? The Willowcroft Prohibition families? This mysterious 'A' character? Are they connected?

The group conversation centered on the local families.

"Eleanor was quite clear. The Walsh, Grey, and Michaels families were as tight-knit as stitches on a quilt. But after the '54 bank heist, accusations flew like needles in a sewing circle," said Mrs. T.

"Which led to a fracture so deep that the Michaels uprooted their lives all the way to Florida," Olivia said.

"Being in the Sunshine State doesn't take them out of our game," said Wally. "And let's not forget the Greys cozying up with Detroit's Adams crime family. They could still be flexing their muscles here in Willowcroft."

"Those muscles might have shattered my store's window," Olivia said. "And there has to be a prior connection between the Greys and Adams for Samuel and Charlotte to meet in the first place."

"And you're sure it's the same Adams family?" asked Tammy.

"In genealogy, the rule is you need a minimum of two or three matching sources before you can claim an ancestor," said Olivia.

"And how many do you have?" asked Wally.

"Two exact matches. The 1950 census has an eighteen-year-old Charlotte Adams in Detroit with her father, Emerson Adams, at the address Wally visited. And on Samuel and Charlotte's marriage certificate, the father of the bride is one Emerson Adams at the same address as the census. That's as clear as you can get."

"The Detroit connections are no joke," Mrs. T said. "If the Adams had a hand in this, we're kicking the dust off a rug they hoped would stay rolled up."

"Which is why we need to be smart about it," Wally said. "Play their game until we know how to win it."

Lockie found Tammy's lap as she sat next to Olivia. "If we're right about the tunnels being more than just booze and speakeasies—"

"Then there's no telling what other lies are buried beneath our feet," Mrs. T finished for her.

"Or who might kill to keep it buried," Olivia added, folding her arms.

A silence settled over the room. Tammy stroked Lockie's soft fur as he purred.

Wally stood and paced. "If Rowe unearthed something, there are people determined to keep it hidden. We need to figure out what it is before anyone else gets hurt."

The front door cracked open. Tammy looked up as Xander barreled inside, his backpack half-zipped and eyes blazing with purpose. "I think I've found out who 'A' is."

"Who?" she asked.

"According to the ISP, it's a Carter Moore." Xander booted up his laptop.

"That name sounds familiar," said Mrs. T.

"Yes, he's mentioned in the guest records you pulled," said Xander.

"He's a descendant living in Florida," added Olivia. "A grandson of Clark Michaels!"

Xander typed as he talked. "When Mrs. T got her list of names from the inn, we only cross-referenced it with Rowe's podcast victims, which we were focusing on."

"What a shame," said Mrs. T.

"Got it!" said Xander. "Remember when we first started seeking descendants? I called someone in Florida, and they hung up on me, saying they wanted nothing to do with it. That was Carter."

"Really?" Olivia raised an eyebrow. "And we thought nothing of it at the time?"

"We had multiple hang-ups and made contact with a different Michaels descendant."

"Emily Michaels, Clark's great-granddaughter," said Wally. "She didn't know anything. She hoped we'd tell her about the bank heist."

"But what does 'A' mean?" asked Olivia. "And why did he ignore us only to reach out to Rowe?"

"Perhaps he changed his mind," Mrs. T suggested. "Or he realized he was stirring up trouble."

"Or he was advised to keep quiet," Wally added, pacing slowly in front of the fireplace.

"By someone in his family," Tammy said, tapping her fingers against her chin.

"Or the Adams family…" Olivia trailed off, her eyes distant.

Tammy reached down, stroking Lockie's fur and drawing comfort from the purring vibrations.

"Maybe he just wanted us to think that," said Wally.

"Playing possum?" Mrs. T said.

"If Carter is 'A' and lured Rowe here, he is our prime suspect," said Tammy. "We need to track him down."

"He might still be at the Inn," said Mrs. T.

"If he was the murderer, wouldn't he have left town by now?" asked Olivia.

Tammy reached for her phone. "Only one way to find out." Dialing the inn's number, she put it on speakerphone so everyone could hear.

"Willowcroft Inn. How can I help you?" Georgina's polite tone came through the line.

"Mr. Moore's room, please."

"One moment."

A brief pause, and then the line connected.

"Hello?" came the unsteady reply.

"Mr. Moore?" Tammy asked.

"Uh, yes. Who is this?" The man sounded nervous.

A flurry of excitement rippled through the team, causing Tammy to shush everyone. They all bent closer, not wanting to miss a single word.

"Um, I'm calling to confirm some details regarding your relationship to Clark Michaels," Tammy improvised.

"Wait, how did you…?"

"Friends of Rowe Harvey," Tammy ventured, watching the surrounding reactions. Wally's cheeks clenched; Mrs. T went still.

"Rowe?" Moore's voice wavered once more, and for a moment, Tammy imagined his pulse throbbing through the line.

"Could we meet to discuss—"

Click.

"Wow," Xander said, breaking the silence. "He's hiding something."

"Or he's scared," Olivia added. "What if someone dangerous is after him too?"

"Regardless, we need to discover why he reached out to Rowe," said Mrs. T.

"We rattled him," Wally said, standing and stretching his legs. "Scared men make mistakes."

"Or scared men tell the truth," Tammy mused, her writer's instinct sensing the plot thickening, the story weaving itself into new, unexpected directions.

"Time for answers," Wally said.

"Is he going to throw a brick through my window now that he knows we're on to him?" Olivia asked, only half-joking.

"It's time I paid Mr. Moore a visit," said Wally.

"Shouldn't we inform the sheriff?" Tammy asked.

"Stanton's already juggling the Adams family connection," Wally dismissed, reaching for his coat. "This needs subtlety."

"Funny, I never thought of slipping out the back as subtle," Olivia said.

"That's because you've never been a cop," Wally countered with a wry smile, easing open the back door enough to slip through.

"But what about Deputy Brown out front?" Tammy asked.

Wally grinned. "What he doesn't know won't hurt him. I'll sneak around him."

"Why don't we tell him?" Xander asked.

"Because he'll either forbid me from going or want to come with me," said Wally. "I don't think arriving at Carter's door with a deputy is the best way to get him talking."

Wally disappeared.

Olivia's lips pressed into a thin line. "What if he gets caught—"

"Then we'll bake cookies for the station and claim it was all part of a fundraising ruse," Mrs. T offered.

"Fundraising for what?" Xander asked.

"Wayward detectives and their meddlesome friends," Tammy quipped, earning a chuckle.

Chapter 23

Certain no one was watching, Wally darted from one tree to another like a seasoned professional. A rush of adrenaline sharpened his focus as he navigated the backyard, avoiding any potential obstacles and monitoring Brown's position.

He reached the fence at the property's edge—higher than he remembered—and hoisted himself up with a grunt. Aging knees protested, but his determination remained solid. After landing with a soft thud on the other side, he brushed off his coat with a sigh.

"Guess I'm not as spry as I used to be." He peeked back to ensure no one had seen his less-than-graceful exit. The coast was clear.

He just had to pass the Hubbards' residence without getting caught by Marjorie during her daily porch sweep, which Wally had nicknamed the "Neighborhood Recon Hour."

After Marjorie's house, it was a straight line to the inn where Rowe had stayed and Carter Moore was staying. A fizzy sort of exhilaration lingered beneath his ribs, part nerves, part satisfaction at having slipped past the deputy and Mrs. Hubbard. He took a moment to catch his breath and smooth out his hair before heading inside.

A man barreled through the lobby, his rapid steps betraying an urgent need to escape. Clad in a flustered mix of travel garments, the man juggled bags too cumbersome for a hasty retreat.

Wally stepped into the man's path, causing a collision that sent the suitcases tumbling and their owner crashing to the floor.

"Carter Moore, I assume?" Wally extended a hand to help him up.

The man flinched at the sound of his name and ignored the offered hand, rising with jerky movements. His shoulders hunched, and his breath quickened as he staggered back a step. "Who are you? What do you want?"

He kept shifting his weight, as if he were gearing to bolt, scanning for exits Wally knew didn't exist.

"Easy now." Wally raised his hands in a placating gesture. "I'm not here to hurt you. I'm Wally, one of the founding members of the Willowcroft Tunnel Museum. I wanted to ask you a few questions, since you are a descendant of a bootlegging family."

Carter's fear abated somewhat, though he eyed Wally warily.

"Is that all?" Carter asked as he adjusted his coat.

Wally nodded, then continued, "I'd also like to know whether you killed Rowe Harvey when you met her in the tunnels."

Carter jolted, shoulders snapping rigid. "She was already dead. I swear. I didn't do it." His words tumbled out in a vehement cascade of denial. In his eyes was the stark terror of a man who stumbled upon a nightmare and could not awaken. "I knew they'd think it was me, so I ran. I had to run."

Carter's face paled. His hands quivered. His eyes reflected the raw panic of innocence wrongly cornered. Wally saw no guilt behind the man's haunted eyes.

Wally's instincts told him the man was telling the truth. Only the innocent acted that scared. "All right. I believe you. But we should discuss this elsewhere." He glanced around the inn's lobby, catching sight of George and Georgina trying to act nonchalant while eavesdropping on their conversation. "These walls have ears."

Carter hesitated, then nodded in agreement.

"Here's the plan," Wally said. "My place. It's safe, and we can talk without interruption." Scribbling directions on a scrap of paper, he passed it to Carter. "Tell Deputy Brown out front you're coming for a visit. He's one of us; he'll let you through."

"And you?"

"Ah, I had to sneak out the back door to get here. I'll take the scenic route home. I'll explain there."

Through the back door, Wally appeared, a little breathless. A chuckle escaped him as he spotted Carter at the table, his presence confirming the man hadn't taken flight.

"Ahh. You made it," Wally said.

Carter gave a nervous smile, his hands fidgeting with the edge of the napkin before him. Two scones later, under the comforting spell of Mrs. Temperance's hospitality, his story unfurled.

"I contacted Rowe," Carter confessed, crumbs clinging to his lips. "I used 'A'—as in Anonymous."

Olivia slumped back in her seat, the drama radiating from her like a wilted flower in a detective noir. "Anonymous? Seriously? I was hoping for arch-nemesis, or agent provocateur, something with flair." She cast a glare at Wally as if he should personally apologize for the letdown.

Carter let a laugh slip out, more reflex than amusement, as his fingers resumed tracing circles on his plate.

Carter explained how he'd seen the story about the discovery of the 1954 bank heist money in the news, along with the mention of a secret back entrance behind fake boxes in the Willowcroft Bank.

"I found a key to a safe deposit box my grandfather left behind. Never thought much of it. I figured whatever it held had lost value years back."

"Yet here you are," Wally said. "Drawn back by the whispers of old ghosts and the lure of a mystery unsolved."

"Exactly," Carter breathed out. "The bank heist money, the tunnels... how did it tie in with my family?" He gripped his knees, then released them. "My grandfather moved to Florida over sixty years ago, but Willowcroft... it never loosened its hold, did it?"

Carter's curiosity got the better of him. He flew to Michigan to access the safe deposit box. It contained his great-grandfather's memoir about the family, including their bootlegging during Prohibition. As he read through the pages, Carter discovered his great-grandfather knew about the secret entrance to the bank, which could have made his family a suspect in the heist.

The pages described a bitter feud among three families who had once shared deep ties—the Michaels, the Greys, and the Walshes. Carter had always known his family had left Michigan under difficult circumstances, but he had never known the details.

"The three families accused each other of orchestrating the robbery and not sharing the money," Carter explained, his voice laced with sadness. "Mistrust and greed tore them apart."

"There was an unspoken agreement not to use the bank entrance," Carter continued. "If it was discovered, they feared prosecution for their Prohibition-era crimes, which would have come to light during an investigation. The memoir makes it clear we did nothing illegal *after* Prohibition, so anything afterward had to be by one of the others."

"Which is why you contacted Rowe Harvey?" Tammy asked, trying to make sense of the tangled history.

"She was the ideal person to do the digging. To discover any wrong-doings and who was responsible, leaving my family forever vindicated as innocent. I never thought it would end in murder."

"Old grudges run deep," Mrs. T said. "Especially when pride and greed are at stake."

Lockie, perched on the windowsill, let out a soft meow, as if in agreement. The group turned toward the sound.

"I never meant for any of this to happen," Carter said heavily. "I wanted Rowe to clear my family's name." He put his head in his hands. "Instead, I set events in motion that ended in her death."

Wally stood to add another log to the fire.

Carter shifted in his seat. "I figured checking out of the inn the same night as the murder would be suspicious, so I stayed and tried to act normal. I knew I didn't kill her."

The room seemed to hold its breath as everyone absorbed Carter's words. He appeared scared and confused, which only added to the complexity of the situation.

"Then Tammy called," he continued, his voice trembling slightly. "I panicked. Maybe it was time to run. So I did, but ran straight into Wally... and now I'm here, eating scones with strangers and telling all my family secrets," he finished with an anxious laugh. "What happens next? I never meant for any of this to happen."

He dropped his head into his hands.

Carter was in a fragile state. It was clear he had never been in a situation like this before and didn't know what to do.

Wally placed a reassuring hand on the man's shoulder. "You're safe here with us, and we'll do everything we can to sort out this mess."

Carter stared at him. "Feels like I'm trapped in one of those old mystery novels. Except I can't flip to the end to read how it turns out."

"I wish life was a book with a neat conclusion," Tammy said.

"What happened on Halloween night?" asked Olivia.

"I had arranged to meet Rowe at eight at the tunnel museum entrance. I stayed in my room until it was time to leave."

"And you were alone?"

"Yes."

"Tell us everything from when you left the inn," said Wally. "You may have seen something without realizing it."

"Close your eyes," said Mrs. T. "Take yourself back to that night and then take us back with you."

Carter drew in a deep breath. "I remember zipping my windbreaker and stepping out into chaos. The square resembled a carnival gone rogue. Kids in capes and bear onesies were tearing through hay bales, parents clutched punch like lifelines, and someone dressed as a haunted priest repeatedly shouted, 'Happy Halloween!'"

He gave a hollow chuckle. "I had to weave through it all, dodging candy apples and plastic pitchforks, trying not to draw attention. I figured if I appeared nervous, I'd be noticed. I kept my head down and my bag close, as if it could somehow protect me."

He opened his eyes. "The edge of town was quieter. Only one flickering streetlight past the bonfire and contests. That's when things shifted. I could no longer hear any music or laughter. Nothing but leaves and wrappers underfoot."

He paused. "I got to the museum around eight, as we had planned. Rowe said she wanted to meet where it all happened. Said she might be able to clear our name."

He swallowed. "The door was open a crack. I'm not sure how she got in. I thought maybe she'd brought someone else with her who had a key. I pushed it."

His gaze fixed somewhere beyond the room. "It smelled... damp. Earthy. I called out for her. Nothing. So I went down, one hand on the rail. The stairs were slick. The air colder."

He held his breath.

"Then I saw her."

Carter's voice dropped. "She was lying at the bottom. For a second, I considered if she was pulling some kind of stunt. Rowe liked to test reactions, saying it made for good audio. But then I noticed the angle of her neck."

"I panicked. Ran." He let out a shaky exhale. "That's it. That's what happened. I didn't touch her. I didn't even get close. I never should've agreed to meet her there."

Wally didn't flinch. He leaned forward, elbows on his knees. It was time for the rapid question round. Too quick for lies.

"Start at the top again. What time did you leave the inn?"

Carter shifted. "Around 7:40. I didn't want to be late."

"You walk the whole way?"

"Yeah."

"You talk to anyone? Anyone see you?"

"The innkeeper. He was handing out candy in the lobby. I didn't stop to chat."

"You didn't drive? You've got a rental."

"The square was closed to traffic for the celebrations. I didn't know another way."

"Yet you arranged to meet her there."

"She insisted."

"Did you notice anyone coming into town on your way out?"

"No, no one after I left the square."

"The door. It was open?"

"Just cracked."

"Did you touch it?"

"No—I mean, yeah, I pushed it."

"You call her name?"

"Twice."

"You didn't spot her when you first started down?"

Carter hesitated. "Not until I reached the bottom of the stairs."

"The door upstairs was open, the light on, and Rowe was already dead?"

"No light. I had to use my phone to see."

"You sure she wasn't alive?"

Carter blinked. "Positive. She wasn't breathing."

"You say you didn't touch her, not even to check for signs of life?"

"No. I couldn't... I couldn't get that close."

"You run back the way you came?"

"Yeah. Straight back toward town."

Wally braced himself. "Anyone else know you were meeting her?"

"I didn't tell a soul."

"You ever been to the tunnel museum before?"

"No."

"Then how'd you know the way?"

"She emailed me directions."

Wally glanced down at his notes, then back at Carter. "Her podcast went out live at 7:25. You left the inn around 7:40?"

"Right."

"Someone was with her while she was broadcasting."

"I didn't hear anything. Didn't see anyone."

"You're sure?"

Carter faltered. "The body blocked out everything else."

"Did you hear footsteps? A door closing? Heavy breathing? Something to suggest you weren't alone?"

"No. It was completely still."

Wally narrowed his eyes. "Did anything seem... off? Out of place?"

Carter rubbed his temples. "The look on her face. Like she'd been surprised."

Wally kept his voice low, but his focus didn't waver. "Last question. When you saw her body, what was your first thought?"

Carter's throat moved as he swallowed. "It was my fault."

Wally didn't write that one down.

"Did everyone take notes?" Wally surveyed the team.

Xander brandished his phone. "I recorded it."

"Good thinking."

"Wow, remind me never to get interrogated by *Detective* Wallace," whispered Olivia.

I've still got it.

"What happens now?" Carter asked.

"You tell your story to the sheriff," said Wally as he sent off a text.

Carter's breath hitched and his spine locked rigid.

"Don't worry." Wally stood, his stance exuding reassurance. "I'll call him over, explain everything. He trusts my judgment."

"Are you sure?" Carter's eyes darted to the window.

"Stanton will need to officially rule you out before you leave town. Standard formalities. Nothing more."

"We were all suspects once too," said Olivia. "And to be clear, you didn't break the window?"

"What window?"

Olivia slumped back in her seat.

Carter glanced down at the scone remnants on his plate. "Formalities, right."

"This is a difficult situation you've found yourself in. But we'll help you through it."

Carter lifted his head. "You believe me then?"

"I was a homicide detective for thirty years. I can spot a guilty man, and you're not one."

Carter sighed, the tension leaving his shoulders.

"The memoir," Wally said. "It suggests the Michaels, Greys, and Walshes go back over a hundred years here in Willowcroft?"

"Near a hundred and fifty according to my great-grandfather's writings."

Chapter 24

"With Carter off the hook," Wally said, "we need to search elsewhere." His gaze connected with each person around the room, seeking silent agreement.

Mrs. Temperance shook her head, her knitting needles clicking in a steady rhythm. "Our best suspect off the list."

"If we had the murder board, I'd cross 'A' off," Olivia said. "Why didn't I bring it?"

"It would look suspicious, dear, wheeling it across the square," Mrs. T said.

Wally processed the facts as he would a case file back in Boston. Carter came to learn what Ms. Harvey had found, but she died before sharing that information. The killer took her phone, which meant incriminating evidence existed on it.

"Let's think about this. The Grey-Adams connection. They have history. And power."

"And we know the Adams have long memories. They wouldn't appreciate Rowe stirring up old dirt, especially not on the eve of those tunnels opening to the public."

Mrs. Temperance continued her knitting without lifting her eyes. "Maybe they're cleaning house, starting with Rowe... and now sending threats our way with Olivia's window."

Olivia gripped her mug tight, her knuckles reddening from the heat. "What did Mr. Adams say?"

"Enough to confirm they're not fans of the woman." Wally kept his face neutral, years of interrogation experience kicking in. "He hinted at consequences for sticking one's nose where it doesn't belong."

Tammy crossed her arms. "So we're next on their list."

Lockie shifted beside the couch, tail flicking once before curling back into sleep. *At least someone felt safe.*

"But the mention of Willowcroft caught him by surprise."

"Sheriff's Department. Don't move."

The shout came from the porch. Loud. Sudden. Unmistakable.

Lockie sprang upright, fur bristling.

A crackling hiss tore through the air, ending in a sharp pop.

Wally flinched.

Carter yelped.

Chairs scraped.

Wally spotted motion in his peripheral vision. Lockie darted under the couch as Olivia straightened and Mrs. T rose, but he raised a hand to steady them.

Then silence.

"Come on out, Wally," came Stanton's familiar tone.

Wally let out a slow breath. The room behind him stayed tense, but that voice was enough for him. His shoulders eased.

He crossed to the door and pulled it open.

Brown was on the porch, handcuffing a man dressed in black from head to toe who lay face down on the boards. A black ski mask sat askew, revealing a young man's furious expression. Nearby, Stanton held a spent taser in one hand.

"What in blazes?" The words slipped from Wally's mouth without thinking.

"I got your message about Carter needing to talk. Found this one skulking around your house, armed and up to no good. Thought it best to take him down."

Wally studied the groaning figure as Lockie crept past him, tail puffed like a feather duster. "Well, I'm glad you stopped him in time."

The deputy lifted the suspect to his feet. The man glared at the group, his eyes burning with anger.

Lockie let out a low growl, his hackles still raised.

"Turns out, the Adams family lives under constant surveillance. I called in a favor with an old friend in Detroit and found out one of their 'handlers'—as in 'heavyweights'—disappeared yesterday." Stanton paused and took a deep breath. "It stands to reason if he smashed Olivia's bookstore window but hadn't returned, he might still be lurking around Willowcroft. And I was right. You poked a big bear."

Wally pictured himself face to face with the bear he'd encountered months ago. Cold dread curled low in his stomach. His life had changed for the better since then, but... "I never want to poke a bear."

Stanton signaled to Brown to take the suspect to the car. "Let's wrap it up." The deputy marched the handcuffed man down the steps with an iron grip.

No one spoke. The porch creaked beneath their shifting weight as Wally's mind worked through the situation like a puzzle box refusing to open. He'd seen enough in his years on the force to know nothing was ever as simple as it seemed.

Carter stood rigid, his face pale and his eyes darting around. Wally assessed him with a long stare. His fists clenched, his jaw tight. Fear, plain as day.

"Let's take this inside," the sheriff said. "There's one problem. Our friend"—he pointed to the squad car—"has a solid alibi for the night of Rowe's murder. Two of Detroit's finest tailed him all night."

"Then someone else is still out there," Mrs. T said.

"Stay vigilant," Stanton said. "I'll need statements from all of you, starting with Carter."

"Can I go home?" Carter's voice shook.

"Sorry. You're coming with me," Stanton replied. "Let's sort this out at the Sheriff's Department."

The sheriff turned to Wally. "Call me if you uncover *anything*."

With that, he guided a trembling Carter outside to the squad car. Wally watched them leave, then closed, locked, and bolted the door. Through the window, Brown's silhouette stood guard.

The team took stock in the living room.

Lockie padded in a slow circle, sniffed Wally's shoe, then hopped onto the couch beside Tammy, nestling against her leg.

"Whoever killed Rowe isn't finished with us yet," Wally said. The perp always circles back, hungry for more.

"Here's to solving mysteries without becoming one." Xander gripped his phone. "I'm calling Park Ranger *Dad* and heading home before this gets weirder. My dad knows how to tame poked bears."

Mrs. T resumed her knitting. "Good thinking. We don't want you, or any of us, to end up like Rowe."

Olivia threw herself onto the couch, her arms flailing like a stage actress at curtain call. "Oh, come on! Are we crossing the Adams family off the murder board suspect list too?"

Chapter 25

Hazel surveyed Wally's living room. It bore the marks of their long night. Mugs perched on every flat surface. Notes carpeted the coffee table, curling at the corners. Lockie batted one across the floor.

The others moved about the room with the heavy-limbed sluggishness of people who had slept poorly. Olivia yawned into her cup. Tammy scrolled through her phone with unfocused eyes. Wally busied himself in the kitchen, the clatter of mugs suggesting another round of caffeine was imminent.

He returned with a fresh pot in hand. "What are you thinking, Mrs. T?"

"Maybe there are clues in the magazine remnants the innkeeper gave me from Rowe's first visit. She probably assumed they'd be thrown out when the room was cleaned, but thankfully for us, they weren't. They might provide hints on what else she was working on if we could figure out the words she cut out."

Wally nodded. "We're assuming the 'Talk or be talked about' letter was made by Rowe for an unknown target."

"This has the Willow-Crafters written all over it," said Mrs. T.

Tammy looked at Mrs. T. "The knitting circle?"

"Puzzles, organization, detail work—they live for this kind of thing," Mrs. T said. "Especially Della Mae. That woman hasn't thrown out a magazine since the '80s. If anyone can help match these scraps to their sources, it's Dell."

Hazel pulled out her phone. "The more eyes on this, the better."

Her thumbs moved across the screen. She'd mastered texting faster than knitting cables, much to her own amusement.

She started a Notty but Nice group chat.

Hazel: Emergency knitting circle. My house. One hour. Curiosity and patience required. No yarn necessary.

Hazel: Della Mae, I need every *Good Housekeeping* issue from the past year.

Della Mae: On it! I've got doubles of the spring ones.

Marjorie: Emergency? Should I come with scones or scoldings?

Beatrice: I'm bringing my sharpest reading glasses. No more raisin scones, Marjorie.

Betty: If there's a mystery involved, count me in.

Marjorie: Fine, I'll bring note cards.

Hazel smiled to herself. That would do.

She tucked the phone into her skirt pocket. "The Willow-Crafters will help solve this puzzle."

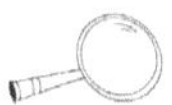

A loud knock rattled the front door. Hazel adjusted her grip on the teacup before it slipped from her hand.

"Coming!" She set the cup in place and hurried to the door.

Marjorie stood on the porch, clutching blank cards. "This better qualify as an emergency. Mrs. Peters's Christmas sweater won't block itself."

"Trust me, it qualifies." Hazel stepped aside.

Beatrice arrived next, soil still clinging to her fingernails. "Came straight from the tomatoes. Hope you don't mind."

"Garden dirt brings good luck. Get in here."

Betty swept through the doorway. "Emergency meetings thrill me to bits. I told Jeffrey, you remember, my third cousin's boy? I said, 'Jeffrey, nothing dull happens with the Willow-Crafters.'"

The porch steps groaned under the weight of an ancient pram Della Mae was hauling, stacked high with magazines.

"Good heavens. The entire collection?"

"You said a year's worth." Della Mae patted the towering pile. "Wasn't sure, so I brought everything this old girl could carry. Doubles as my compost hauler."

"You're magnificent." Hazel guided her inside.

She briefed them on the case developments before explaining their mission. "Ladies, our knitting takes a backseat today. Rowe Harvey left these cut-up periodicals during her first visit, weeks ahead of the tunnel opening. If we decipher what she removed, we uncover what Rowe never lived to tell."

Marjorie inched forward. "Something scandalous?"

"A secret romance." Betty fluttered her eyelashes.

Marjorie's eyes rolled. "Let's work."

Beatrice adjusted her glasses. "So we compare Della's intact copies against Rowe's ravaged ones?"

"Exactly." Hazel distributed the magazines. "Five of us will crack this puzzle."

Betty flipped through a tattered issue. "Like those movie ransom notes."

"That's our theory." Hazel laid the materials out across the table.

Each woman claimed part of Rowe's collection and matched it with Della Mae's pristine version.

The room fell silent except for the rustle of pages.

"Found one!" Betty jabbed her finger at a Crock-Pot recipe. "The 'F' is missing here."

Della Mae slapped her magazine down. "This beats our mystery novel. Got a 'T' cut from page seventeen."

"And an 'A' gone from this fall centerpiece feature." Marjorie marked the spot with her finger.

Hazel placed corresponding Scrabble tiles on the table for each discovery.

"I've got G, O, L, and I from this single article," Beatrice said. "Goli? Logi?"

"Logical?" Betty suggested.

"Nothing about this is logical," Marjorie muttered.

Letters were called out as they were found.

"P."

"D."

"S."

"Spy!" said Betty.

"There's no Y," said Marjorie.

Della Mae piped up. "I've got your Y."

"And an N," said Marjorie. "Yarn!"

"Why would she be spying on yarn?" asked Betty.

"She can't with only one Y. And before you say it, I don't think Rowe belonged to a knitting circle spy ring either," said Beatrice.

"Why not?" asked Betty. "Isn't that what we are now?"

Hazel arranged the scattered tiles and tried to rein in the conversation. "Look what we've found."

F T A R H E G O L I P S Y N D

"Fat—she's body-shaming someone!" Betty bounced in her seat, hands flailing as she pointed at the letter pieces. "Do you see it?"

"Keep searching." Hazel shifted the letters.

Their voices overlapped as they rearranged possibilities.

"Party."

"Safety."

"Fires."

"Pirates."

"Fear."

"Heart."

Della Mae rotated several tiles, nudging them into a new line.

"Here's more." Marjorie tapped a page. "She cut 'BIO' from biography."

"And 'Grey' from this Earl Grey tea advertisement." Beatrice added.

"I've found an 'OPT'," said Betty.

Della Mae continued to rearrange the tiles: F A T H E R. "Add BIO to LOGI—"

"And consider adding A and D to OPT," Hazel said.

"Biological father," Marjorie's voice dropped.

"The GREY family," Hazel whispered.

Betty pulled another clipping. "She removed 'Ams' from Amsterdam."

Her mind stumbled, trying to catch up. "Adams?"

"A note about her biological father," Marjorie said. "Connected to the Adams and Grey families."

Heat rose in Hazel's face as connections fired in her brain. "Rowe didn't come for the tunnel story. She came hunting her roots."

"So she was adopted?" Betty asked.

"Potentially." Hazel gathered the reconstructed message. "And she believed her biological father was linked to the Greys or Adamses."

Beatrice gave a slow whistle.

The scattered magazines—decades of homemaking advice that had provided raw materials for Rowe's private quest—seemed suddenly poignant.

A young woman searching for family had turned to *Good Housekeeping*, the very emblem of hearth and home.

"We've uncovered her true reason for visiting Willowcroft." Hazel lifted her lukewarm tea. "And why she was silenced."

Marjorie crossed her arms. "If only we could connect one of the Adamses to the murder."

"Their alibis are airtight," said Hazel. "Police were tailing them all in Detroit throughout the night."

Della Mae frowned. "They couldn't be in two places at once."

"No." Hazel set down her cup. "But men with that kind of money buy more than sports cars."

"They paid someone off." Marjorie's voice sharpened.

"Power rewrites rules." Hazel tasted bitterness in her mouth. "We assume police reports contain the truth. Some truths have price tags."

Silence blanketed the room.

Beatrice reached for a cookie. "You hope good people wear the badges."

"Most do," Hazel said. "Takes just one willing to turn a blind eye."

Betty deflated against her chair. "The worst part is not knowing who to trust."

Hazel's fingers tightened around her cup. "This changes everything. I need to tell the others right now."

Chapter 26

As soon as school finished, Xander made his way to Olivia's bookstore, where the window was being replaced. Olivia was "supervising" Mike the glazier out front, and Tammy was lollygagging with a bowl of nuts, staring at the murder board.

He combed through Rowe's emails again to find more clues. Had he missed something?

Xander clicked on the trash folder. Empty. Who empties their trash unless they have something to hide? It hit him. Hidden in plain sight. Maybe the names on the folders didn't reflect what was inside.

His eyes darted around the screen, scanning for a new angle. For the most part, she had an organized labeling system. But one stood out: "Domestic News America." Why include "America" and "domestic"? Wasn't that redundant? Suspicious. Worth a look.

The folder contained lab reports from Deep Roots Genetics.

Dozens of results appeared. Only one confirmed a match. A father-daughter relationship.

"There's more going on than we thought."

Olivia peeked her head through the door. "Any leads?"

"The plot thickens!" Xander declared, unable to contain his excitement. "Rowe has a folder of DNA tests."

Olivia settled beside him. "Her next big scoop?"

"It must be. There are no names, but plenty of samples. She was tracking down someone's family secrets with multiple candidates."

"DNA can tear everything you thought you knew apart," Olivia said.

Tammy joined them, brushing peanut shells from her hands. "I knew there was another layer!"

"Illegitimate children," Olivia said with relish. "She uncovered connections no one wanted found."

"Do you use DNA in your genealogy stuff?" Xander asked. "Like, how does it all work?"

Olivia pushed back a strand of curly hair. "Some genealogists do, but I haven't ventured into the DNA side yet. Old-fashioned paper trails for me."

Xander nodded, absorbing this. "But you'd know, right? If a person was trying to track family ties through DNA?"

"It's something I'd love to learn more about," Olivia replied.

Tammy tapped her chin. "Whoever it was knew there was a connection—but not who the link was to until that one report."

"It's a great motive for murder," Xander said.

"Where did she get the samples?" Olivia studied the reports. "I'm no expert, but the female one appears to be the same each time."

"So she was searching for someone's father," said Tammy.

Mrs. T bounded through the secret bookshelf door. "We did it! The Willow-Crafters did it!"

"Calm down, Mrs. T. What did you find?" asked Olivia.

"The letters Rowe was writing with the cutouts from magazines were about finding her biological family. We think Rowe was adopted."

"Adopted!" Xander ran a hand through his hair. "She was trying to find *her* father. The female samples were all hers, and she was testing them against possibilities."

Tammy's eyes grew wide. "She didn't know which family she belonged to, but they might have known. It would explain why they wanted her gone."

"What are you all talking about?" asked Mrs. T.

"Rowe had a collection of DNA results from a private lab," said Xander. "Did she have permission for those samples?"

"I'm guessing not," Wally's voice boomed as he walked in, shaking off the cold. "If she was the one who rummaged through the Adams' bins a few weeks back, then she could have found all sorts of things with DNA on them—a drink bottle or toothbrush."

Tammy's mouth dropped open. "You think Rowe was an Adams?"

"Biologically possible," Olivia said.

Wally took a seat. "Would explain their strong reaction."

"She found them, and they found her," Mrs. T added with dramatic flair.

"Bet they didn't want word getting out," Xander said, his eyes like saucers.

Tammy clapped her hands together. "If Rowe knew—"

"She'd have had quite the story," Olivia finished.

Wally surveyed them with approval. "We're onto something big."

Olivia tapped a pen against the table. "How do we confirm what she found without meeting the same fate?"

"But we've cleared the Adams family," said Tammy.

"The Willow-Crafters considered crooked cops," said Mrs. T.

"Please, no," said Wally. "I need pie."

Chapter 27

Wally went next door to the Swinging Spoon and ordered a slice of Peggy's finest. There's nothing he hates more than dirty cops.

"Need a refill there?" Peggy approached with a fresh pot.

"Wouldn't say no." He pushed his mug forward. "Got a lot to chew on besides your cherry pie."

The bell above the door jangled. Councilman Evan Dean marched in, tie askew and normally slicked-back hair disheveled.

"Coffee. Black. To go." Dean barked the order, his attention never leaving his phone.

Peggy stilled, eyeing him with the kind of flat stare Wally had seen her use on rowdy teenagers and short-tempered tourists. She reached for a to-go cup and set it on the counter with a deliberate clack, louder than necessary. The councilman glanced up and locked eyes with Wally. Dean's face hardened. Color drained from his cheeks.

"Never mind," Dean snapped, shoving the phone into a pocket. "I'm late for an appointment."

He turned on his heel and stormed out, the door slamming behind him.

"What in blazes was that about?" asked Wally. "He practically sprinted across the square."

Peggy snorted. "That man's got the manners of a junkyard dog. You'd think being elected would require basic courtesy."

"He seemed mighty concerned to see me sitting here."

"Huh." Peggy topped off Wally's cup. "Speaking of our esteemed councilman, can you believe he tried to shut down your museum project? Fought it tooth and nail from day one."

Wally's detective instincts perked up. "He was vocal against it, wasn't he?"

"Vocal? The man lived at town hall, filing objections. Cost concerns, disruption to tourism, historical inaccuracies. You name it, he claimed it. Said the money should go to fixing the square instead." Peggy wiped down the counter with more force than necessary. "That poor Rowe woman knew all about him."

Wally squared his shoulders. "Ms. Harvey? How so?"

"They had quite the heated discussion right here, the day she died. She was asking him questions, and he didn't much care for them."

"Did you tell Stanton about this?"

Peggy pressed her lips together. "I clean forgot until now. Dean's always grumpy with folks. A lot of people disagree with his voting record on the council. Didn't seem unusual at the time. It was Dean being Dean. I hadn't registered it was with Rowe on the day she died."

"What exactly did they talk about?" Wally kept his voice casual. Had Dean felt threatened by Rowe's questions? Was she getting too close to something?

"Let's see…" Peggy leaned against the counter. "She had that little recorder of hers out. Asked him why he was so dead set against the tunnel museum. He said something about it being a waste of taxpayer money on 'fabricated history' and 'town gossip.'"

"Fabricated history? The tunnels are right there under our feet."

"That's what she said!" Peggy pointed her dishrag at him. "But I heard from Katie, who heard from Marjorie, who heard directly from Elsbeth over at town hall that Dean was going through the archives, trying to find evidence against what your team uncovered."

Wally frowned. "He wanted to disprove that Prohibition happened in Willowcroft?"

"Yes! Something about it all being lies, and the town would be the laughingstock of the state if they went ahead with a public museum based on that version of events."

"How in the name of all that's holy did he think he could prove Prohibition didn't happen? We've got the tunnels, the speakeasy, historical documents—"

"I guess he couldn't, and that's why the project went ahead." Peggy refilled a regular's coffee cup down the counter before returning. "He did mumble something about families."

"Did he mention any names?"

"None I recall. But he said something odd." Peggy lowered her voice. "He said we were 'tarnishing the reputations of good people.' Got real defensive when Rowe pressed him on it."

"That's suspicious," Wally muttered to himself.

"Oh! And he made some kind of threat. Told her there'd be 'consequences' from the tunnel project." Peggy shook her head. "I thought he meant political consequences, you know? But now with her being murdered..."

Wally pulled out his wallet and laid a ten-dollar bill on the counter. "You said Marjorie heard from Elsbeth?"

"That's right. Elsbeth as in the town hall secretary. Been there forever."

"And does Bev from the sheriff's department happen to be friends with Elsbeth?"

Peggy's eyes lit up. "Why, yes! They've been bridge partners every Thursday night for as long as I can remember."

Wally stood up, his mind already mapping out his next steps. "I need to pay Bev a visit."

"You think Dean might be involved in what happened to Rowe?"

"Let's examine the facts." Wally counted them off on his fingers. "She was investigating family connections to Prohibition. Dean was adamant the museum not go ahead. They argued shortly before her death. And now he storms out of here when he sees me."

"You still have a detective brain."

"Some tools never get rusty." Wally headed for the door. "If anyone asks, I'm following a hunch."

It was time to use his "in" with Bev.

Please let it be Dean rather than dirty cops.

Chapter 28

Wally used the side entrance of the sheriff's building, which led to Bev's domain.

"Mr. Wallace! What brings you back to the scene of the crime?" Bev peered up from the computer, reading glasses perched on the end of her nose. Her workspace was as tidy and precise as he remembered.

"I'm here to cash in that promise you made at Mary Collins's grave." Wally braced himself against her desk. "You said I could get into the archives if the time ever came."

Bev's fingers paused over her keyboard. "I remember. What are you after this time?" She opened the top drawer to retrieve the key.

"The situation's evolved." Wally lowered his voice. "I'm looking into a lead in the Rowe Harvey murder. It ties back to the council. I need access to the town hall records."

"And the sheriff's okay with this?" She raised an eyebrow.

"Let's call it a parallel investigation." He flashed the smile that had gotten him out of trouble with his ex-wife more times than he could count. "Your friend Elsbeth might be required this time."

Bev removed her glasses. "You've been doing your homework."

"Peggy mentioned bridge."

"Thursday nights for fifteen years." Bev pursed her lips. "What are you looking for?"

"Information on what Councilman Dean might have been using to stop the museum from opening."

"This is about the tunnels?"

"It is now." Wally tapped his fingers on the desk. "Evan Dean fought the project like it was going to expose nuclear launch codes. Then Rowe Harvey starts asking questions, and she turns up dead in the tunnels."

She stared at him for a long moment. "I'm not supposed to tell you anything pertinent to an open investigation—"

Stanton's blocking me? "But?"

"I did see Dean's name in relation to the case. A witness mentioned he'd fought with Ms. Harvey."

Someone from the diner reported it.

Bev reached for her phone. "Let me call Elsbeth. She's working late tonight, cataloging old council minutes."

Wally was in luck. Elsbeth would let him in at six.

Evenings in the Town Hall carried the kind of silence that made Wally's shoulder blades twitch. Too quiet. Like secrets hung in the drywall. Elsbeth met him at the front entrance, keys already in hand, lips pressed thin.

"Bev said you're assisting the sheriff."

"In a manner of speaking. Tying up loose ends."

She nodded once and led him down the side hallway. Her steps were soft but purposeful, like someone used to moving through government buildings after hours. They passed closed doors and then descended a narrow staircase.

Elsbeth unlocked the heavy door at the bottom and flicked on the overhead light. The archives room sprang to life.

"Everything's labeled. Took me six months to sort it. Council records are on the east wall, organized by decade," Elsbeth pointed out. "Family records—births, deaths, property titles—are on the north wall. Minutes and voting records are in those filing cabinets. There's a computer at the desk. It's temperamental, but it has an index of everything and access to the scanned documents. The older stuff is still in the original files."

"Any records about the Dean family?"

She hesitated. "Councilman Dean? Why the interest in that family?"

"I'm covering all bases for my research. The family's been on the council for generations."

"Evan's the third Dean to serve. His grandfather, Howard, held office the longest, though I believe 'Dean' was his stepfather's name."

Wally forced a neutral expression. "Do you happen to know his birth father's name?"

"It will be in here somewhere." She waved her hand around as if to say good luck finding it.

"How about Prohibition records?"

"West wall, bottom shelves. Some are in rough shape. Water damage from the flood in '83. Marjorie knows all about that one." Elsbeth winked before checking her watch.

"You've got two hours. I need to prep council packets upstairs."

Note to self: ask Marjorie about the flood. There's a story there.

Wally moved toward the desk. The green-shaded lamp cast a tight circle of light. Dust coated the keyboard. The computer grumbled to life after a few clicks.

He started with the search function. Dean, Evan. Too many records. Council minutes, permit applications, event attendance logs.

Dean, Howard, the name Elsbeth mentioned. That produced council notes from the seventies, but nothing about family origins.

Birth certificates? The database showed restricted access. And anyway, how do you find a birth certificate without a name? Wally drummed his fingers on the desk.

Think. If I can't find the beginning, start from what I know.

He tapped the edge of the keyboard, hoping for inspiration.

Personnel files.

Not the usual place for family history, but if Dean was a sitting councilman, there'd be a file. A resume. Worth a shot.

He typed: Dean, Evan—Personnel.

"Access restricted." The error message glared at him.

Wally tried again, typing: Dean, Evan—Public Office.

One entry appeared.

The PDF loaded slowly. A scan of forms filed with the town clerk when Dean took office. Most fields contained standard information, but a notation caught his eye: "See attached legal name documentation."

Bingo.

He opened the attachment. A single-page affidavit. At age twenty-four, Evan Bishop had legally changed his name to Evan Dean. Reason given: "To honor my stepfather, Mark Dean, who raised me."

Wally stared at the screen.

Bishop, not Dean.

He jotted the full legal name down in his notebook: *Evan Franklin Bishop*, born to *Franklin Bishop III* and *Dorothy Wilcox*, 1975.

Wally eased into the backrest, pen suspended mid-air.

Why change it?

Plenty of folks took a new name for show—stage names, easier spelling, that sort of thing. But a local councilman doing it in his twenties? Smelled like cleanup. Burying a trail.

He wanted to block the museum. He'd fought it. Hard. Was there a connection?

Wally turned back to the keyboard. This wasn't about Evan anymore. This was about his first family.

He backed out of the personnel folder and entered a new search: Bishop, Franklin. Dozens of hits. He scrolled until he saw one labeled *Council Minutes, 1956—Bishop, Franklin II.*

Wait. III? II? How far back does this go?

He clicked "Print" and rose from his chair as the printer near the door hummed to life.

He cleared the search bar and typed: Bishop—Prohibition.

The screen froze, then went black. Wally smacked the side of the monitor. Nothing.

"Great."

He pushed away from the desk and strode to the west wall, squatting down to examine the boxes Elsbeth had indicated. The labels showed years—1920-1925, 1926-1930, and so on. Wally pulled the first box free, dust clouding the air. He carried it to the central table and lifted the lid.

Inside, yellowed papers and folders sat in neat rows, separated by dividers. He flipped through several holding building permits, liquor citations, council minutes.

There wasn't time to read them all. He flicked through, hoping something would jump out at him.

Among the newspaper clippings, handwritten notes, and official-looking letterhead documents, one article caught his eye: "Local Businessman

Franklin Bishop Appointed to Town Council." The accompanying photo was grainy. But the jawline? That arrogant tilt to the head? Pure Dean.

Wally rubbed his chin. So the Bishops were in government before the Deans even entered the picture.

He pulled a fresh page from his notebook and jotted a list.

Franklin Bishop Sr.—councilman, 1920s

Franklin Bishop Jr.—property deal in the 1950s?

Franklin Bishop III—Evan's father. Died young.

Evan Bishop—now Evan Dean

Four generations. Three kept the name. One buried it.

Wally returned to the box. Nothing triggered a connection. He replaced the first box and pulled the next one from the shelf, repeating the process.

In the third, he hit paydirt. "Land Reclassification, 1920-1925." He scanned through the brittle pages, stopping at a council meeting agenda from 1922.

"Proposal submitted by Councilman Franklin Bishop Sr. to reclassify Parcel 14B and adjoining lots near the riverfront as restricted public access due to 'erosion concerns and unsafe terrain.'"

Wally glanced at a town map hanging on the wall. Parcel 14B bordered what was now state park land.

He dug deeper into the folder, finding a deed from six months after the reclassification. It showed a transfer to a man named Iverson Adams.

His brain snagged on the name.

He froze, staring at the signature on the deed. Adams. Not Emerson, the one he'd met two days ago, but Iverson. The man who had made the family name infamous in Detroit during Prohibition. Wally pulled out his phone. A quick internet search confirmed his suspicion that Iverson was Emerson Sr.'s father.

Got you.

He carried the deed to the printer, fumbling with the old photocopier beside it. The machine wheezed but produced a copy. He returned to the files.

A pattern took shape. Two years later, another parcel along the river. Reclassified for "public safety," then sold to Ronald Adams. A cousin or brother? It didn't matter. It was an Adams.

The computer screen flickered back to life. Wally hurried back to the desk, typing another search before it crashed again. Budget records from the 1920s. Luck struck. Bishop Sr. had pushed through a special allocation for "riverfront maintenance and security." The funds went to a private contractor: Adams Freight & Timber.

He hit print as the machine froze again.

Wally scribbled frantically in his notebook.

Bishop rezones land, makes it off-limits, Adams buys it cheap. Then Bishop allocates town money to the same company. Public funds into private pockets.

It explained why Dean opposed the tunnel museum. Digging into history could have exposed his family.

The Bishops enabled the Adams operation and profited from it. And Evan Dean, born Evan Bishop, carried that legacy.

He returned to the file boxes, pulling more documents on land transfers. Each one connected the Bishop family to the Adams family. He shuttled between the photocopier and the filing cabinets, gathering evidence.

The Adamses bought people in power. And they kept the public away from what they didn't want them to know.

Legacy protection. Wally wrote the words in the margin of his notebook.

Dean's name change. His anxiety. His opposition. None of it was about civic duty.

It was about hiding the rot in the family tree.

He gathered his photocopies and printouts and slipped them into a manila folder he'd found in the desk drawer. Wally placed the folder securely into his small canvas knapsack and zipped it closed.

The computer screen blinked off with a low whine as Wally organized his materials.

Upstairs, a chair scraped against the linoleum. A door slammed.

He moved toward the stairwell.

Elsbeth met him at the top. "Find what you needed?"

"Just scratching the surface, but I've got some good material." Wally tucked his notebook into his pocket and adjusted the knapsack strap. "Out of curiosity, could anyone walk in and request those files? Say... a podcaster? Tourist? Historian?"

She laughed. "Officially, yes. Unofficially? Not a chance. The archive room stays locked. I don't allow anyone down there without proper authorization."

"So if someone *had* seen those records..."

"They'd have needed someone to vouch for them. Why?"

"Making sure I didn't waste a favor." He patted his knapsack. How did Rowe get access? "Has anyone been down here recently?"

"Thomas Berry brought someone down a month or so ago. He's always in and out doing research for the Gazette."

He's been Rowe's contact from the start.

Elsbeth glanced toward the hallway. "You might want to use the side exit. Councilman Dean arrived a moment ago. Saw him heading to his office."

Wally paused. "Dean's here now?"

"Yes, third door on the right." Her gaze lingered, as if testing his reaction. "Problem?"

Wally weighed his options. Confront Dean now with what he'd found, or regroup with the team first? Instincts honed from years on the force told him to gather more evidence before revealing his hand.

"No, but I'll use that other exit you mentioned." He smiled. "Appreciate the heads-up."

Outside in the cool evening air, he pulled out his phone. He typed a text to the team:

> **Wally:** Councilman Dean's grandfather Franklin Bishop was on Adams's payroll. Dean at town hall now. You all at my place? Brown there?

> **Tammy:** All here. Deputy on duty outside. What's happening?

> **Wally:** Heading home. Calling Stanton now.

Wally punched in Stanton's number as he walked the short block to his house.

"Stanton."

"I've got something on Rowe Harvey's murder. Evan Dean is connected to the Adams family going back to Prohibition. Evidence of payoffs, corruption. She might have discovered it."

"Where are you now?"

"Walking home from Town Hall. Just left the archives."

"I'll come to you."

"I'm almost out the fr—"

A blow from behind sent Wally stumbling forward. His phone clattered to the sidewalk. The knapsack slipped from his shoulder and fell beside him. He spun around, fists raised by instinct, to find Councilman Evan Dean advancing on him.

"You couldn't just leave it alone." Dean's face contorted with rage. "Had to keep digging into things that don't concern you!"

Wally squared his stance. "Murder concerns everyone, Councilman. Especially when it happens in my town."

"She was going to ruin everything!" Dean lunged forward, swinging. "Exposing my family!"

Wally blocked the punch and shoved him back. "So you killed her to keep your family's dirty laundry hidden?"

"She wouldn't back down!" Dean charged again, catching Wally with a glancing blow to the ribs. "I won't let you drag my grandfather's name through the mud!"

They grappled on the sidewalk, Dean's fury compensating for what he lacked in technique. Wally, despite his age, had muscle memory from decades of police work. He pushed Dean off and created distance between them.

"Freeze!" Deputy Brown's voice cut through the night as he sprinted toward them from the direction of Wally's house.

Dean ignored the command, diving at Wally again. They crashed into the old oak marking the corner of Marjorie Hubbard's yard.

"What in the name of all that's decent is going on out here?" Marjorie's garden gate banged open. The seventy-five-year-old woman emerged in her bathrobe, brandishing a broom like a medieval weapon. "Evan Dean! Have you lost your mind?"

Dean had Wally pinned against the tree, hands gripping his collar. "You don't understand what's at stake!"

"I understand you're assaulting a citizen in front of an officer." Brown drew his taser. "Step back now."

"And on my property line!" Marjorie added, advancing with her broom. With surprising speed for her age, she swung it, catching Dean across the shoulders with a solid thwack. "You ought to be ashamed, a public official carrying on like a common thug!"

The unexpected attack from Marjorie gave Wally the opening he needed. He twisted free from Dean's grip and swept the councilman's legs from under him. Dean hit the ground with a grunt.

Brown moved in, handcuffing the councilman as he struggled. "I'm arresting you for assault, sir."

"He's ruined everything like the podcaster tried to do!" Dean shouted, straining against the cuffs.

Wally spied the team on his porch.

Marjorie adjusted her robe with dignity, broom still in hand. "I've lived across from Wally for twelve years, and he's the most decent man in this town. Whatever he's found on you, Evan Dean, I'd bet my pension it's the truth."

A squad car pulled up, lights flashing. Stanton stepped out, taking in the scene. The deputy restrained a struggling councilman. Marjorie was poised with her broom, and Wally brushed dirt from his jacket.

"What did I miss?" the sheriff asked, approaching Wally.

"Mrs. Hubbard saved me from Dean here." Wally rubbed his jaw where the councilman had landed a lucky punch. "But I think we got our confession."

Dean's face paled. "I never said I killed her!"

"No," Wally agreed, "but you admitted she 'tried' to ruin everything. Past tense."

As Stanton led Dean to the squad car, Wally retrieved his knapsack and the phone that had fallen to the ground. The screen was cracked but still functional. Inside the bag, a manila folder held solid proof of a family legacy steeped in corruption. It was the very evidence Rowe Harvey had been on the verge of exposing.

The team descended from the porch, gathering around him with questions in their eyes. Wally looked from their concerned faces to Marjorie's triumphant stance with her broom to Deputy Brown's professional demeanor.

"Who wants hot cocoa?" he asked. "I've got a doozy of a story to tell."

Chapter 29

Tammy walked the floor of the Sheriff's Department waiting area in uneven steps. Steady movement might signal calm she didn't feel. No one appeared sure of anything. Xander stared at his phone without moving his thumbs. Olivia perched on the armrest beside Mrs. Temperance, lips pressed tight, not saying a word. The older woman's knitting sat limp in her lap, needles stilled as if even they didn't know what to do. Marjorie Hubbard rearranged the community brochures again. Third time? Fourth? She'd lost count.

The inner office door swung wide.

Sheriff Stanton stepped out, rubbed a hand over his face, then folded his arms. "He confessed."

Tammy halted mid-step.

"Dean admitted to killing Rowe." Stanton's voice was steady, but the fatigue showed in the slump of his shoulders. "He claimed she was planning to destroy his family's name. She said her podcast would unravel three generations of the Dean legacy. Or rather, the Bishop legacy. If it ever aired."

Mrs. T released a quiet sigh.

The front door crashed inward. The community bulletin board rattled in response. Della Mae raced through with Betty huffing behind her.

"What are you two doing here?" the sheriff asked.

"Marjorie posted on the Knotty But Nice group chat that you were all here. We wanted to come too. We helped."

Stanton rolled his eyes.

"Was someone else involved?" Olivia asked.

The sheriff shook his head. "No. He acted alone. Nothing suggests an accomplice. No cover-up team. He hoped it would be deemed an accident. A fall down the stairs."

"From the live podcast, we know there was a struggle," Tammy said.

"Dean said once she fought back, he snapped. Called it instinct. Rage."

Xander lifted his focus from his phone. "All that... to hide a name on a council record?"

"It wasn't just that," Stanton replied. "It was the story she planned to tell. The Adams family's dirty money. The corruption. The deals hidden for nearly a century. His whole life existed on the illusion his family served the town. Rowe Harvey wanted to shatter that."

"People will destroy anything to preserve their version of history," Mrs. T said.

"What time was Ms. Harvey killed, Sheriff?" Marjorie asked.

"Around seven twenty-five based on her podcast."

Marjorie sniffed, then poised herself in her chair like a woman about to announce a pie contest winner. "Well then, I'm afraid Mr. Dean's confession is pure hogwash."

Tammy's mouth fell open. Hogwash?

"I can give Evan Dean a solid alibi," Marjorie said, brushing an invisible crumb off her lap. "He didn't do it."

Of all the people to derail their theory, Marjorie Hubbard ranked last on her list of suspects.

"He stood on the town hall steps giving out the prize for best children's costume," Marjorie continued. "Seven-thirty sharp every year."

"I can vouch for the timing," Della Mae said. "When the announcement started, I checked my watch. We were in line for the chili guy. We'd been waiting since seven."

Tammy shifted her weight and folded her arms across her chest. Wait. What?

"Roger has to eat at seven or he turns vicious," Della Mae added, flinging her hand. "The sign said 'Back in five,' but he was gone much longer. The costume awards kicked off at seven-thirty, like always, and I remember thinking we hadn't budged. I was shocked Roger hadn't keeled over from hunger. We got pasties from the stall next door instead."

"Wait," Tammy said. "The chili guy. Big man, orange apron, cooking out of a cauldron?"

"That's him."

"I interviewed him, Mr. Garrett from Ann Arbor. Rowe recorded a podcast episode about his brother. He showed me photos to prove he stayed at the stall all evening. They had timestamps between six thirty and ten."

Della Mae scoffed. "Well, I guarantee he vanished from seven at the latest to after seven-thirty. My husband's stomach keeps perfect time."

Tammy fell back against the wall. Dean couldn't have killed Rowe. Did the chili man lie? "But Lockie accompanied me."

At his name, the cat lifted his head from where he lounged beside Olivia and stretched.

"He sniffed Mr. Garrett's pants leg and walked away. No hiss, no bristling. And Lockie usually knows."

The cat padded over and brushed her ankle.

Tammy glared down at him. "Did the spices confuse you? Disrupt your killer radar? Or were you still under the influence of valerian?"

Lockie meowed once and settled by her feet, curling into a neat black-and-white ball, as if that was all the answer Tammy needed.

"I'll search through social media posts," Xander said, his fingers springing to life on his keyboard. "Maybe I'll find a photo showing the stand empty."

"Are you questioning me, young man?" Della Mae glared.

"Ooh, Thomas Berry," Betty interjected.

"What about him?" Stanton asked.

"He took photos all night. I bet he captured evidence in one of his pictures."

"Yes," Della Mae said. "I think he took one of us while we waited in line!"

"Brown," Stanton barked with sudden urgency, "call Ann Arbor PD. I want everything they have on Mr. Garrett. Background, license plates, any priors. And send a deputy to the Berry household. If Thomas photographed all night, we need those images now."

The deputy reached for his radio. "On it."

Della Mae frowned. "Why would a man from Ann Arbor serve chili here?"

Tammy caught her breath. "Garrett told me his college roommate came from Willowcroft..."

The rustle of shifting bodies filled the room as heads swiveled in Tammy's direction.

"Could it be Councilman Dean?" she whispered, conviction strengthening with each word. "Maybe Garrett came as a favor. And when Dean realized what his friend had done... he attempted to cover for him."

Silence blanketed the room after Tammy's words.

Stanton rocked back on his heels. "If your theory holds, we have a false confession and a killer free."

Olivia stood. "Then we need proof. Fast."

Xander stared at his phone. "Already found blurry shots from the town square. Chili stand might be empty in one of them."

Mrs. T grabbed her knitting again, needles clicking in time with the renewed urgency in the room. "Let's hope Thomas's photos show something clearer."

Tammy glanced at Lockie. She dug her fingernails into her palm.

"Do you think Dean knew Rowe's real reason for visiting town?" she asked. "Not the tunnels or the council... but the adoption?"

Lockie's ears flattened.

"Adoption?" The sheriff snapped upright, hands landing on his hips. "What adoption?"

The knitting needles in Mrs. T's hands stopped. "We haven't shared everything yet."

Tammy moved closer to Stanton. "Rowe's research suggested she was adopted and her birth family had a connection to Willowcroft."

A muscle jumped in Stanton's cheek.

"Rowe believed she could be related to the Adams family," Olivia added. "She sent DNA tests to a private lab."

"The Adams robbery where nothing disappeared," Wally said. "We think she took something from their trash for DNA testing, like a toothbrush—"

"Or hair," the sheriff interrupted. "We found envelopes with strange items, like hair, in her room. We couldn't determine why."

"Hair provides perfect DNA samples if the bulb is attached," Olivia said.

Stanton rocked back on his heels. "The Adams family wouldn't welcome long-lost relatives appearing suddenly."

"But we know they didn't kill Rowe," Wally said.

Stanton's phone pinged. He checked the screen, then signaled Deputy Brown. "Ann Arbor PD forwarded Garrett's file. A confrontation occurred with Ms. Harvey, but no charges or restraining orders resulted. A neighbor called the police."

"Garrett has motive, which prompted our interview," Tammy said. "I thought I verified the timestamps on his photos, but he must have flipped through them too fast for me to spot the gap." She bit the inside of her cheek. She should've caught it.

"If we can prove where he went when he left his chili stand, we might have him," said Stanton.

"Does my word count for nothing?" Della Mae huffed.

The interrogation room door opened. Evan Dean emerged between two deputies, his shoulders slumped but his chin high.

"Your testimony proves his absence from the stand, but we need to establish his location to charge him with murder."

"I confessed." Each word tore itself from Dean's raw throat, leaving him wincing. "Why won't you listen?"

Tammy stepped forward. "You were presenting awards. The entire town can verify your whereabouts." She pressed, "Your friend Mr. Garrett knew what Rowe planned to expose on her podcast, right? About your family's connections to the Adams syndicate."

Dean's face contorted. "What?"

"The Adams syndicate," Wally repeated. "Your family's connection to them."

Dean stumbled backward until his shoulders hit the wall. "How—" His voice cracked. "How could you know that?"

Stanton exchanged glances with Tammy. "So it's true?"

"My grandfather conducted business with them in the fifties, and my great-grandfather before that." Dean's gaze skittered across the room, never landing on one person for more than a heartbeat. "That podcaster appeared with questions and threats."

He slumped. "I thought my confession would stop the investigation and bury the truth." His eyes found Tammy's. "But no, I didn't kill her."

Stanton's radio crackled. He listened, then addressed the room. "State police stopped a vehicle matching Garrett's description at the county line. Troopers are bringing him in."

"He must have learned about Dean's arrest," Xander suggested, still scrolling through festival photos. "News travels fast."

Thirty tense minutes crawled by. Lockie alternated between pacing and staring at the door. The knitting group whispered theories. Dean sat motionless in a corner chair, hollow-eyed.

When the front door opened, Garrett's bulk filled the frame. Two state troopers flanked him. His face registered surprise at the crowd, then settled into careful neutrality.

"What's this about?" he asked, his eyes finding Dean across the room. "Evan? You okay, buddy?"

"Mr. Garrett." The sheriff stepped forward. "Glad you joined us. We have questions about your whereabouts during the Halloween festival, specifically between seven and eight."

Garrett's smile stiffened. "My stand. Serving chili."

"Not according to witnesses." Stanton gestured to Della Mae.

"There was a sign," she declared. "Back in five minutes. But you vanished for much longer."

"Bathroom break," Garrett shrugged. "The porta potties had lines. And anyway, you're not a cop."

"No, but I witnessed your absence when Ms. Harvey died."

Deputy Brown approached with a printout. "Sheriff, Thomas Berry's camera timestamps everything. This shows 7.20." He handed the photo to Stanton. "That's Della Mae and Roger Beasley. Chili stand clearly empty behind them."

Della Mae beamed. "Told you Roger's stomach keeps perfect time."

"And this one shows 6.45," Brown continued, handing over a second image. "Garrett appears in the background of the apple bobbing competition, outside Pippa's Pop-Ins, facing away from town."

Tammy set her shoulders. "Pippa's sits on the path to the museum. If he left then, he had time to reach it."

Another deputy called out. "Councilman Dean's phone records show a call to Garrett at six thirty-five."

Stanton tilted his head. "What transpired during that conversation?"

Betty raised her hand like a schoolchild. "That's after Mr. Dean dropped his candy bucket."

"Correct," Marjorie added. "Ms. Harvey mentioned something about council minutes, and the bucket crashed to the pavement."

"And then the petunias and the unicorn incident," Betty said.

Stanton raised his hand. "Ladies, please."

He turned to Garrett. "Hand over your phone."

The man nodded and reached into his coat pocket. He produced a device and offered it without resistance.

The moment the sheriff took it, his brow creased. He angled the screen toward himself and then positioned it toward the light.

Olivia leaped forward. "That's not his."

Tammy squinted at the locked screen. Her breath caught. A familiar image stared back at her of a stylized microphone over a swirling purple background. Rowe's podcast logo.

"That's Rowe Harvey's," she said.

Garrett froze.

No one moved. No one breathed. Even Lockie's tail stopped its rhythmic sweep across the floor.

Stanton lifted his gaze and waited.

Garrett's hands twitched. He patted his coat again, more frantic now. Another phone emerged from an inner pocket, and he thrust it forward as if it proved something.

"This one," he said. "This is mine."

Stanton remained still. "Why do you possess Rowe Harvey's phone?"

The trap snapped shut. No escaping now.

Lockie crept closer, ears flattened against his head. A low growl rumbled from his throat as he moved toward Garrett.

"Rowe had her phone when she left the inn. George saw it," Wally said.

"And investigators couldn't find it at the crime scene," Tammy added.

Stanton's head snapped toward them. "How do you know that?"

Tammy opened her mouth, then closed it again.

Wally cleared his throat. "I might have spoken with George."

The sheriff's jaw tightened. "You what?"

"And I might have overheard deputies talking at the crime scene, which is on my property."

Stanton exhaled through his nose and stared skyward as if pleading for patience. "Of course you did. Why do I bother telling you to stay uninvolved?"

Lockie's growl intensified, his eyes locked on Garrett.

Stanton pointed at the two of them. "We'll discuss this later. For now, someone log these phones into evidence and find out what else he's hiding."

Garrett's eyes darted between faces, calculation visible behind them. "I found it." He delivered the words without inflection, his face a blank mask. "At the festival. Lying on the ground."

Tammy didn't move. No one did. *Seriously?* He still thought he could lie his way out?

"The ground," Stanton repeated. "At the festival."

"That's right. When I was at the bathrooms." Sweat beaded on Garrett's forehead.

Tammy stepped forward. "Did you find it before or after you placed the 'back in five' sign at your chili stand?"

Garrett's Adam's apple bobbed. "I don't recall a sign."

"But you remember finding a phone?" Stanton pressed. "We can place you outside Pippa's Pop-Ins, and that's the opposite side of the square from the porta potties.

Garrett's shoulders sagged, his face crumbled. His eyes landed on Dean, who sat motionless, staring back with a vacant stare.

"Evan," he whispered. "I'm sorry."

Lockie hissed, his back arched, fur standing on end as he positioned himself between Tammy and Garrett.

"Now you're telling me he's guilty," Tammy said.

Garrett stepped back from the cat. "She destroyed my family. I refused to let her ruin Evan's too."

The room froze.

"She produced a podcast about my brother digging up old wounds. People shunned him. He never recovered." Garrett's face flushed, his tone raw. "Then Dean called me, frantic. Said Rowe asked about council minutes, that she uncovered the Adams syndicate connection. He sounded desperate. I recognized it in his voice. And I knew if she published her findings, his life would collapse too."

Garrett swallowed hard and balled his hands into fists. "So I contacted Rowe. Claimed I had proof of corruption and offered to help. Suggested meeting at the tunnel museum to hand it over."

A sour taste filled the back of Tammy's mouth. She pressed her palm against her abdomen.

"Too many people crowded the square for Halloween. The tunnels offered privacy. They were secluded, shadowed, and away from foot traffic." Garrett's words came out hoarse. "I picked the lock. My brother taught me. I waited in the dark."

He stared at the floor. "She entered. I heard her call out, asking if someone was there. I thought she spotted me, and if she recognized me, she might run. I panicked."

He inhaled sharply, then words spilled out in a rush. "I struck her. Just swung. She fell. I fled, grabbing her phone, assuming it contained her evidence." He paused. "I entered some kind of shock. I've never killed before. I forgot I had it until now."

Stanton blinked at him, then released a long, gruff breath. "Two confessions for the same murder in one night." He rubbed the bridge of his nose. "I'll need gallons of coffee and a miracle to complete the paperwork."

He turned to the amateur detectives and onlookers. "Everyone who doesn't have a badge or is called Garrett or Dean, please exit the building and allow the professionals to work."

Marjorie sniffed. "Typical. We crack the case, and it's time for us to clear the room."

Wally shrugged, hands tucked smugly in his coat pockets. "At least I don't have to fill out the reports. Perks of retirement."

Olivia rose with a weary smile. "So what now?"

Wally scratched his chin. "I vote for pancakes."

Chapter 30

Olivia smoothed the wrinkled newspaper clipping before placing it in the evidence box. Their murder board offered a sorry display, with only a handful of index cards and photos on it behind the secret bookshelf in her store's back room. They'd abandoned their usual headquarters for Wally's house during much of the investigation.

"I can't believe Garrett killed Rowe for Councilman Dean." Tammy coiled a length of red yarn they'd used to connect suspects. "He seemed more annoying than dangerous."

"Some predators hide behind the blandest masks," Mrs. Temperance replied, labeling a folder with her elegant handwriting.

In the corner, Xander hunched over his laptop, fingers flying across the keyboard. "I'm downloading all the evidence files to our secure server. In case."

Lockie attacked one of her crumpled notes, his tail flagging in victory when it fell to the floor. The small moment of normalcy brought a welcome smile to her face.

The distinctive sound of the bookshelf mechanism turning made Olivia's head snap up.

Sheriff Stanton's head appeared first, followed by his broad shoulders as he ducked through the doorway. He paused, blinking as he scanned their hidden workspace.

"Had to try three different shelves before I found the right one." He tugged his uniform straight. "I knew there was a door somewhere."

Olivia set down her box, heat rising to her cheeks. Their secret lair was exposed.

"So this is where you play detective." The sheriff zeroed in on the murder board.

Mrs. T straightened her spine. "We prefer 'concerned citizens who assist law enforcement.'" She then sat in the comfortable chair and picked up her knitting.

Stanton pointed to the half-dismantled display. "Looks like you're wrapping things up."

"We assumed the case was closed." Tammy crossed her arms.

"It is closed," he confirmed. "We got the full story from both Dean and Garrett by the early hours of this morning."

"And," said Olivia, "you haven't come just to tell us that."

"No, no." He inhaled deeply. "Dean claims Ms. Harvey approached him in private. Showed him everything she'd found. Told him she was an Adams by blood. Said she was publishing the lot from the family corruption to her own connection to the legacy."

"And Dean couldn't let that happen," Wally said.

Stanton hesitated. "He panicked, but he wasn't the one who acted. Dean called Garrett, shaken after Rowe confronted him again at the Halloween festival. Something in that call pulled Garrett back. To his brother. To everything Rowe had already torn apart."

Olivia's stomach tensed. The trial. The fallout.

"According to his statement, hearing Dean unravel was the breaking point." Stanton paced behind the chairs. "It brought everything flooding back. What Rowe's reporting cost his family."

"So this was revenge?" Tammy's eyes widened.

"In a way." He stopped moving. "Garrett couldn't bear watching his college roommate go through the same downfall."

Wally whistled low. "Talk about misplaced loyalty."

"To use the man's own words"—Stanton mimicked quotation marks with his fingers—"he wasn't brave enough to defend his brother back then, but he wouldn't let her destroy another life."

No one spoke. Olivia held her breath without meaning to.

"He didn't tell Dean," Stanton continued. "It was a spur-of-the-moment decision. Called Rowe at the inn, claimed he had something important to show her, left the chili stand, killed her at the tunnels."

"And then what?" Olivia needed more details.

"He returned to the square and insisted every customer have a photo with him, hoping the crowd would cover the gap in his timeline."

Tammy snorted. "Not exactly criminal mastermind material."

Stanton shook his head. "Roger Beasley's stomach came in handy for once."

"Where does Carter Moore fit into all this?" Tammy asked.

"Pure coincidence he'd been in touch with Rowe and arranged a meeting at the same location an hour later."

"I bet that doesn't sit right with those who don't believe in coincidences." Xander shot a pointed look at Wally.

Stanton cleared his throat, as if shifting gears. He glanced around the cluttered back room. "By the way, have any of you seen a small figurine? That fluffy white lamb, about this big?" He held his hand a few inches above the table. "Used to sit on the front desk at the station. It was there yesterday, and now it's vanished."

From her place beside Mrs. T, Olivia caught the subtle change. The older woman's knitting needles paused mid-air, her hands suspended as if caught between instinct and thought.

Wally chuckled, his eyes on Stanton. "Lamby? Don't tell me someone's made off with Lamby."

"You know I hate that name," Stanton said with a grimace.

"Three generations of Willowcroft sheriffs have called it Lamby," Wally replied. "Before we all started digging up cold cases and turning our quiet town upside down, the most exciting thing we dealt with was finding missing pets. And Lamby never failed us there."

"Which is why I'd like it back," Stanton said. "Mrs. Peters's tabby has gone missing, and Lamby's always been our good luck charm for finding strays."

"No," Mrs. T said, her tone steady as she resumed her knitting. "I can't say I've noticed it. Have you looked under the desk?"

Olivia tilted her head slightly. The response was unremarkable on the surface, but something about the timing struck her. She glanced at Tammy, who was distracted by Lockie, and then at Xander, still hunched over his laptop. No one else seemed to catch the flicker of tension.

Stanton let out a tired breath. "Probably just a prank. Or someone borrowed it for luck."

"Or," Wally said with mock seriousness, "someone stole it to jinx your animal rescue operations. You know the old saying—'When Lamby's not around, lost pets can't be found.'"

"That's not a saying, Wally. You just made that up," Stanton said, rolling his eyes.

Mrs. T wound her yarn tighter than necessary. "People will take anything not nailed down."

Olivia scrutinized her closely. The needles were moving again, but there was a stiffness in the way her shawl shifted on her shoulders. As if she were bracing for something. But what?

She made a mental note: a missing lamb figurine, a flicker of tension, and Mrs. T—always composed—faltering for just a second too long.

Stanton sighed and returned to the matter at hand. "Anyway, Rowe's research has stirred up a lot about Willowcroft's past that still requires digging into. We're thinking of setting up a taskforce to deal with it."

"What happens to the museum now?" Mrs. T asked, her composure fully restored.

"That's up to you all," Stanton said. "But I think Rowe would want her discoveries to be part of it."

Olivia stroked Lockie's fur. "We'll make sure of it. Her story belongs beside Mary and Cathy's."

"And the town deserves to know," Wally added.

"We're going to need a bigger museum if the body count keeps climbing," said Olivia.

Chapter 31

The rich scent of pine wafted through the store as Olivia struck a match to the candle beside the register. She held the matchbook a moment longer than necessary.

November first had come and gone. The first of the month had always been her quiet signal that the season had begun. For fifteen years, she'd been the first in town to serve hot apple cider when the calendar changed. Two weeks ahead of any other business. It was a small ritual, but one that mattered to her.

The murder investigation had thrown everything off. She was behind. Still, she refused to skip it.

A burst of cold swept in from the front door. The flame trembled.

Olivia turned slowly. Her usual smile waited, ready to greet a regular hunting for a cozy weekend read or a hot spiced drink.

A greeting sat ready on her lips.

She saw who it was.

The words died in her throat.

She hadn't expected him.

Mike the glazier walked in, all windswept hair and easy confidence, holding a small tool kit and wearing that navy fleece she absolutely did not think about more than was reasonable.

"Oh," Olivia blurted, then cringed. "I mean—hi. Hello."

"Hey," he said, the corners of his mouth lifting just enough to make her heartbeat thump in her ears. "Thought I'd pop in and check the window."

She blinked. "Is there a problem?"

"Nope," he said, already strolling toward the front of the store like he belonged there. "But the forecast's calling for a cold snap and maybe snow, so I figured I'd double-check the seal. Make sure you stay warm in here."

Warm was not the issue.

"Oh," she said again, because apparently her vocabulary had collapsed into a single syllable. "That's... very thoughtful."

He crouched beside the frame with a flashlight and traced the edge with steady fingers. She focused on anything but the way his forearms flexed or the soft whistle drifting from him, relaxed and unhurried.

"I don't usually get surprise maintenance visits," she said, aiming for casual. "Is this standard glazier protocol, or something you reserve for frequent flyers?"

Mike glanced up. The corners of his eyes crinkled. "Loyalty perk. And I haven't bought a book since the mystery with the lighthouse on the cover."

"You said you finished it in one night," she replied, the words escaping faster than she intended.

"Quick reader. Repeat seal-checker," he said with a grin.

Olivia's cheeks burned.

Mike stood and tapped the glass. "No drafts. You're sealed tight."

"Good," she said, her voice suddenly too loud. "Great. I mean... we wouldn't want books flying off the shelves in a blizzard."

He chuckled. "Definitely not. Although it would make the news."

She gripped the edge of the counter, grounding herself before her nerves could get the better of her. "Thanks for stopping by."

He lingered like he wasn't quite ready to leave. The quiet stretched long enough to feel deliberate, as if he knew she was flustered and enjoyed it.

"Anytime. If you need anything, even something not made of glass, let me know."

Mike walked to the door and paused, hand on the handle.

"Try to stay warm," he said. "You seem like the type to forget a scarf."

And then he was gone, the bell tinkling softly behind him.

Olivia didn't move. Her breath snagged somewhere between a sigh and a swoon. Her heart did something entirely unscheduled.

She gazed at the window. Still perfect. Crystal clear.

Like the view of Mike walking away.

Olivia shook herself back to reality. The wax had burned down a full inch while she'd stood there, daydreaming like a teenager. She nearly forgot about meeting the others. She flipped the sign to "Back Soon" and hesitated at the coat rack. The diner was literally next door, but grabbed her scarf anyway.

She reached for the door handle, then paused. The candle. With a muttered curse, she turned back and crossed the room to pinch out the flame between her fingers. Fire safety first. Fantasies about glaziers second.

"Oh!" she gasped, smacking her forehead. "The research." She hurried back to the counter where she'd left her folder of notes. She knocked over a stack of bookmarks as she reached across. "Perfect," she grumbled, crouching to gather them.

Standing up too quickly, she banged her hip against the counter. "Oh biscuits, that hurt!" She rubbed the spot that would surely bruise. She did a quick mental inventory, checking that the sign was flipped, the candle out, research gathered, scarf on, before reaching the door again.

Her hand was on the doorknob when she patted her pocket. "Keys," she whispered, spinning around to scan the cluttered counter. She spotted them next to the register and snatched them up, jingling them triumphantly. Taking a deep breath to compose herself, she stepped outside and locked the door behind her.

The November air barely had time to nip at her cheeks before she stepped into the Swinging Spoon. The diner buzzed with conversation, voices pitched just above whispers as locals shared theories about Councilman Dean, Garrett, Rowe Harvey, and the Adams family. Two days had passed since the arrests, but Willowcroft's appetite for gossip remained insatiable.

"I heard the Adams family's sending lawyers from Detroit," a woman at the counter told Peggy as she refilled coffee cups.

"Well, I heard Rowe Harvey's podcast network is planning a special memorial episode," her companion replied.

Olivia slipped into the team's usual booth, where Mrs. Temperance, Tammy, and Lockie were already waiting. Xander arrived moments later, laptop tucked under his arm, and Wally completed their circle, sliding in next to Mrs. T.

"Town's still talking," Wally observed, nodding toward the pair at the coffee station.

"Can you blame them?" Tammy reached for the menu. "A town councilman's college roommate murders a podcaster to hide generations of corruption. Truth is stranger than fiction."

"Except real people were hurt," Mrs. T said. "Rowe may have been brash and ambitious, but she was also chasing something deeply personal."

Peggy approached with a pot of coffee. "The usual for everyone?"

After she'd taken their orders and moved away, Olivia produced the folder. "I spoke with Thomas Berry at the Gazette. He's been digging into Rowe's background since she first contacted him. Her adoptive parents died when she was in college. No siblings. No close friends. Colleagues described her as driven but private."

"Lonely," Mrs. T translated. "Searching for roots."

"And she found them," Wally said. "But not in the way she hoped."

Peggy delivered their food, lingering a moment longer than necessary. "Sheriff stopped by the council meeting last night. Said you all were instrumental in solving the case."

"We followed the evidence," Olivia replied.

"Well, people are saying the museum is more important than ever now." Peggy lowered her voice. "A real testament to telling the truth about our history, no matter how uncomfortable."

Carter Moore approached their table.

"I hope I'm not interrupting," he said. "Stanton has given me permission to leave town, and I wanted to thank you all before returning to Florida."

"Join us," Mrs. T gestured to the space beside Olivia.

Carter slid into the booth. "I heard about Councilman Dean and the chili man."

"Power and reputation can be strong motivators," Wally said.

"That's why I came to see you." He pulled a package from his coat. "Here's my great-grandfather's memoir about Willowcroft during Prohibition. It'll help with your museum."

Olivia opened it. Inside were yellowed pages covered in faded handwriting.

"He mentions everyone from the Walshes to the Bishops to the Adams family operations," Carter added. "How they pressured local businesses and bought off politicians. My family left town because they refused to cooperate."

"These are incredible primary sources," Mrs. T said. "Thank you for sharing them."

"It seems right that the truth should be told," Carter replied.

After lunch, the team walked to the museum. The "CLOSED AS PER SHERIFF'S DEPARTMENT DUE TO MURDER INVESTIGATION" sign had been removed. They replaced it with "REOPENING SOON—EXPANDED EXHIBITS."

"I never expected our museum to become the center of such drama," Tammy said, unlocking the door. "I need to clean the chili off the door. I noticed the red smudges the day I found Rowe's body, but it never occurred to me it was chili and could have led me straight to the killer."

"You hadn't heard of Garrett then," said Olivia. "You could never have made the connection."

Inside, the main exhibition room remained undisturbed. Photos of Mary and Cathy smiled from the wall, their tale preserved for visitors to discover. In the corner, a blank space was the perfect location for Rowe's story.

"She came searching for her past," Olivia said, touching the empty spot. "And in a way, she found it."

Xander placed his laptop on the information desk. "I've drafted some text for the new exhibit: 'Rowe Harvey, descendant of the Adams family, whose search for truth and identity brought her to Willowcroft and ultimately cost her life.'"

"Perfect," Mrs. T nodded. "Simple but meaningful."

A sharp crack split the air.

From the rocky tunnel ceiling above, a jagged icicle broke loose.

It plunged downward and skewered Marjorie's owl pumpkin.

The carved eyes caved in. The sides burst. Orange pulp oozed across the table like something out of a horror movie.

Nobody moved.

Olivia examined the mess, then glanced overhead.

"Maybe we shouldn't open until summer."

Chapter 32

By late afternoon, Olivia found herself back at her store, arranging a display of new historical mysteries. The bell sprang to life, and a woman, relying heavily on a cane for support, entered.

"Miss Huddlestone?" the woman asked. "I'm Barbara Adams Mallinson. I believe you have an interest in my family history."

Olivia recognized the name from the extended family tree she had developed. "Mrs. Mallinson, yes. We've been researching the Adams connection to Willowcroft's Prohibition era."

"And to Rowe Harvey," Barbara added. "She visited me in my assisted care facility last month. Told me she was my great-niece."

Olivia gestured toward the comfortable leather armchair by the front window. "Please, have a seat. Would you like some hot apple cider?"

Barbara nodded and eased into the chair. Despite being over eighty, she sat with impeccable posture, silver hair swept into an elegant chignon that screamed old money.

Outside, the rain had washed the square clean. Now snowflakes spiraled past the lamplight pooling around them, a strangely fitting backdrop for long-buried truths. Olivia set two steaming mugs on the table between them.

"Did you know?" Olivia asked.

"That my niece Elizabeth had given up a baby for adoption? Yes." Barbara's voice held firm. "Our family has many secrets, my dear. Some we keep out of shame, others out of love."

Olivia hesitated. "And Charlotte Adams was your sister?"

"Charlotte was the middle child. Always the wild one. She settled in Willowcroft after marrying Samuel Grey. They lived here for the rest of their lives. She's Rowe's great-aunt too, like me."

Barbara withdrew a folder from her handbag and eased out a wedding photo. She ran her thumb along the edge before offering it to Olivia. "By the early nineties, with both Charlotte and Samuel passed and their children long since scattered, no one with Adams blood remained in town. Until Rowe came knocking."

"Did Charlotte know about the bootlegging operations?" Olivia asked.

Barbara's gaze drifted to the window. "What my father told me as his daughter differs from what Samuel and Charlotte might have shared as husband and wife. Charlotte always had a knack for uncovering things Father tried to hide." She tapped the folder. "I suspect she knew far more than I did."

The elderly woman produced a faded image of two sisters, young and smiling. She pointed to the smaller of the two. "That's me. The baby of the family."

"Would you be willing to share your stories? For our museum?"

Barbara smiled, the lines around her eyes deepening. "That's why I'm here. Rowe started something important. I'd like to help finish what she began."

"I should have come forward sooner." Barbara placed the manila folder on the table. "But family secrets marinate for decades, and the Adams clan specializes in keeping things buried."

"Rowe went her whole life not knowing."

"Her mother, my niece Elizabeth, was nineteen when she got pregnant in 1991."

Barbara showed a photograph of a young woman with Rowe's penetrating eyes. The resemblance made Olivia shudder.

"Elizabeth met Timothy Wright at Northwestern. He was a journalism student. Brilliant. Ambitious. Fearless." Barbara tapped another photograph showing a handsome Black man in his early twenties, leaning against a brick wall with a reporter's notebook in hand. "The Adamses didn't approve."

"Because he was Black?" The question burned in Olivia's throat.

Barbara's expression flattened. "Partly. But mostly because he was investigating corruption tied to our family businesses. Elizabeth fell hard for him. She loved challenging what the family stood for."

The irony sizzled in Olivia's mind. "So Rowe inherited her journalistic instincts from both sides."

"Timothy never knew. Elizabeth's parents shipped her to a private facility in Chicago when she started showing. My sister-in-law Margaret arranged the adoption through her connections. Told her daughter the baby died during childbirth."

Olivia's stomach twisted. "That's monstrous."

"The Adams family cookbook has always included recipes for cruelty disguised as protection." Barbara pulled out a birth certificate. "Rowe Elizabeth, born June 12, 1991. Adopted three days later by the Harveys."

"Did Elizabeth ever learn the truth?"

"She died in a car accident in '99. Never knew her daughter lived." Barbara's voice cracked. "Margaret kept tabs on Rowe through the years. Paid for her education through shell companies and trusts. Even occasionally sent birthday cards signed 'from a friend.'"

"And Rowe came to Willowcroft following her father's journalistic footsteps without realizing it." The pieces snapped into place like a well-documented ancestry record.

"Timothy settled in Chicago after graduation and became an investigative reporter focused on systemic corruption. Made quite a name for himself before cancer took him in 2015."

"Did Rowe ever meet him?"

"Not that I know of. But she admired his career and referenced his work a few times in her episodes."

"You listened to her show?"

"Of course I listened to my great-niece's podcast. I'm old, not dead."

"Sorry. I was impressed with how closely you followed her life."

Barbara handed Olivia a newspaper clipping. The headline read: "Wright Uncovers Decades of Political Misconduct," with a photo of an older version of Timothy accepting a journalism award.

"Rowe deserved to know her history," Barbara said. "Now all I can do is ensure the truth is shared properly."

Olivia's hand paused halfway to her cider mug. "The tunnels and Prohibition weren't just professional leads for her. They were a subconscious journey home."

"Family pulls us back, even when we don't know we're being summoned." Barbara's eyes glistened.

Barbara patted the folder with a worn hand. "Don't worry about the rest of the Adamses," she said firmly. "I'll deal with the family, especially my nephew Emerson. They won't refuse me. I've outlived everyone who could."

Olivia found herself impressed by the woman's determination. There was something formidable beneath Barbara's fragile appearance, a quiet endurance shaped by decades of navigating family politics.

A small, satisfied smile crossed Barbara's face. "It's time Rowe was acknowledged. I'll make sure you have everything you require."

Barbara adjusted her posture. "This is truly a Willowcroft story, as Timothy's extended family still lives here. They have deep roots that date back before the Civil War. They were part of the—"

The bookstore doorbell sprang to life as Tammy and Xander burst in, their cheeks flushed. "Olivia, you won't believe—"

Chapter 33

The cider mugs slammed against the counter with a satisfying crack matching the anger boiling inside Olivia. "Do you have any idea what you interrupted? That woman is nearly ninety. I had to send her into the snow because you came crashing in like a pair of banshees."

Lockie slunk in beside Tammy, his tail lashing back and forth as if sensing the tension.

Tammy flinched. "I—I didn't think—"

"No." The word shot from Olivia's mouth like a bullet. "You didn't."

A beat passed. Tammy's attention shifted to the front of the store. "Oh no. Is it actually snowing?" She stepped closer, fogging the glass with her breath. "I've never seen it fall before. I was so distracted—"

Tammy stood transfixed, staring outside at the swirling white. The urge to snap at her again rose in Olivia's throat, but she swallowed it down.

She tapped her foot against the floorboards. "So?"

Tammy jerked around, cheeks flushed, eyes wide. "Sorry. We couldn't wait."

"Wally's discoveries in the archives have revealed so much more about the tunnels." Xander slipped off one of his backpack straps. "Remember how I said there were tunnels we had seen but weren't marked on the map?"

"Vaguely." The word came out flatter than intended. "And?"

Tammy abandoned the window, Lockie trotting after her like a furry shadow. "Let's go to the back. I brought everything with me."

Without waiting for a response, she made her way to the hidden door tucked behind the shelf. Olivia sighed and followed them through. She grabbed three fresh mugs and the cider jug from the kitchenette's counter. The warm glass doing little to thaw her irritation.

Papers and books spread across the worktable like an academic explosion. Lockie leapt onto the surface, sniffed an open folder, and planted himself squarely in the middle of it.

Olivia distributed the hot drinks, the spicy aroma rising with the steam. "This better be good."

Tammy huddled over her mug. "It is. I've been reading the Michaels Prohibition book you bought, and I've been comparing it with Carter's great-grandfather's memoirs. They each had their own maps."

Xander's laptop screen glowed with the tunnel map. "Wally found council minutes about altering the state park's borders and multiple dubious land sales around town." He pointed at various locations. "They all correspond with potential exits, and it's bigger than the Walsh map. Their map only showed the areas they were responsible for, so to speak."

Tammy flipped to a marked page. "Here. A Michaels descendant said in an interview, 'Grandfather often spoke of the Walsh-Michaels-Grey alliance as the perfect criminal trinity. The Walshes provided the raw materials from their farmland, such as corn and grain. The Michaels family converted them into liquor through our stills hidden throughout the county. And the Greys handled distribution and finances, laundering proceeds through their legitimate businesses.'"

A sheet of notes slid across the table as Lockie shifted. Olivia lunged forward, but Tammy caught it first and nudged the cat aside.

Xander jabbed at a paragraph in the memoir. "Each family had its own zone. Listen, 'The tunnel network was divided by a gentleman's agreement. The western passages belonged to the Walshes for storage, the eastern section housed the Michaelses' distillery operations, and the northern tunnels served the Greys' distribution needs with exits in the park so deliveries would remain hidden. All three connected beneath the town square, including the passage leading to the speakeasy and the Willowcroft Bank.'"

"They all knew about the secret entrance to the bank and swore never to use it for non-'business' related reasons," said Tammy.

"Looks like we're settling in for the night," said Olivia. "I'll order food."

Tammy continued reading from the memoir. "'After the 1954 heist, accusations flew between the families. Walsh accused Grey of breaking their code. Grey blamed Michaels. Michaels suspected Walsh. Blood oaths were broken, and the alliance shattered. Within a month, Clark Michaels packed himself off to Florida.'"

Olivia took the book from Tammy, finding the passage she remembered. "It's mentioned here too." Olivia flipped several pages. "'Clark Michaels severed ties with Willowcroft though rumors persisted of ties to mobster s.'"

"That's where the Adams connection comes in," Xander said. "Samuel Grey married Charlotte Adams in 1956."

"I know all this." The irony of the situation crashed over Olivia. "That woman you made me kick out into the snow was Barbara Adams, Charlotte's sister."

Tammy's mouth dropped open. Xander blinked as if he hadn't processed the words, then slunk back in his chair.

"You're kidding," Tammy breathed.

"No." The word hung sharp in the air. "She came here to talk. To help us. And you two burst in like wild things and drove her out into a snowstorm."

Xander looked stricken. "We didn't know—"

"Exactly. You didn't know." Olivia gulped a breath, trying to dam the flood of frustration. "She brought records, photos, a birth certificate." She took a sip of cider. "Rowe was adopted. Her real parents were Elizabeth Adams and Timothy Wright, who made a name for himself exposing political corruption."

Xander stared. "Wait—*the* Timothy Wright? The award-winning reporter?"

Olivia nodded. "He never knew she existed. The family erased both of them. It was deliberate, cruel, and all too familiar for the Adamses."

Tammy set her mug down. "And Rowe... followed in his footsteps."

"Without knowing a thing." The tragic poetry of it all tightened Olivia's chest. "She had it in her blood, and it led her straight into what they tried to bury."

Tammy and Xander sat frozen. Even Lockie, now curled on a pile of folders, sensed the shift in the room.

"The irony is brutal." Tammy raised her cider. "She came searching for her roots and found them tangled in the corruption she relished exposing."

Xander closed his laptop. "Do we include all this in the museum?"

Truth versus secrets. The answer seemed obvious now. "Haven't we learned that keeping secrets only hurts more people?"

"Rowe would have wanted the story told," said Tammy.

A loud knock startled them.

"Pizza delivery."

Chapter 34

Pine boughs had crept across Willowcroft, replacing jack-o'-lanterns on stoops and swallowing every porch rail in evergreen garlands. Twinkle lights looped around lampposts where cobwebs had fluttered a couple of weeks ago. Olivia cradled a warm mug of cider and watched as winter laid claim to the town.

Tammy hadn't moved from the back door in ten minutes, breath fogging the glass, scarf tucked beneath her chin. Lockie weaved lazy figure-eights at her feet, thoroughly ignored.

White flakes drifted in slow spirals, softening rooftops and streets in layers of quiet hush.

"You know it's the same stuff as this morning, right?" Wally raised his drink. The mug clicked faintly as it touched his teeth.

Tammy didn't look away. "Sure, but isn't every flake a different crystal shape? And besides, it feels thicker now. Like powdered sugar on a gingerbread house."

Olivia gave her cup a gentle swirl, releasing the familiar blend of cinnamon and cloves. In Manhattan, snow transformed into blackened slush that soaked through boots and splashed pant legs. Here, the whiteness lingered. Bright. Clean.

Xander's keyboard clacked in the corner. "It's frozen water."

"That's what makes it magic." Tammy's voice floated back dreamily.

Mrs. Temperance's knitting needles clicked in rhythm. "You should've witnessed her delight when she discovered it made a crunchy sound underfoot."

"She dragged me across the square three times." The memory tugged at Olivia's lips. "Back and forth."

"Worth it," Tammy murmured.

"You've never experienced a proper winter before moving here?" *She's kidding. Right?*

Tammy spun around. "Not in person. Just in movies. And one awful layover in Chicago, which doesn't count because I never left the airport."

"You poor sun-soaked Los Angelino." Wally handed her a warm mug, steam curling between them. "Here in Willowcroft, the first snow means slippery porches, pine-scented everything, and a town that slows enough to notice the difference."

"I'll take it." Tammy faced the glass again, breathing misty shapes against its surface. "Every single flake."

Mrs. T pulled a tin from her tote and opened it with a soft snap. The buttery scent of ginger cookies drifted out as she offered the contents to the group. "The best season for spinning tales indoors."

Lockie stretched, then padded away from Tammy's boots. He settled beside Olivia and tucked his paws neatly beneath him. A slow blink followed, his expression unreadable, as if unimpressed by all the fuss. Earlier, he had watched Tammy marvel and squeal at the falling snow through the front window. His silhouette had barely shown through the frost. Now, he appeared content to claim the coziest spot in the room.

"The tunnel museum's officially closed." Olivia placed her drink on the table with a firm clink. "The final report arrived this morning. With ice formations in the ceilings, it has been deemed too dangerous. A summer reopening is suggested after extensive building work."

"Probably for the best." Wally shifted in his seat. "It was one sharp icicle away from another obituary."

Their laughter bubbled up but faded quickly. Olivia's fingers drummed against her mug, the rhythm matching the questions still tapping at the back of her mind. Rowe's murder had an answer. But everything lurking beneath Willowcroft? Not even close.

"Rowe almost found her family and exposed the Adamses." Tammy stepped away from the door at last.

Mrs. T's needles paused mid-stitch. "Now we must finish what she started."

"We're not done." Olivia's attention drifted to the murder board standing empty in the corner. "There's more buried in this town than anyone guessed. More names. More stories." She clenched her fist against her sternum. "They're here, pressing on my ribs."

Xander closed his laptop with a snap. "We make a good team for amateurs."

Wally shot him a look. "Speak for yourself, kid."

The room brightened with laughter, easier this time.

Mrs. T tucked her knitting into her tote. "The Willow-Crafters are coming over this afternoon. I promised blueberry scones and a fresh theory."

Tammy crouched to scoop up Lockie, who purred and nestled into her arms. "My edits are demanding attention. My fictional sleuth insists I rewrite half a chapter now she's spotted what I missed." She stroked Lockie's fur. "And this little detective needs a snack."

"Homework," Xander muttered, stuffing his laptop into his backpack.

Wally pushed to his feet. "Video chat with my grandkids. They demand I dress as a turkey. I refused. Their mother overruled me. Guess who's wearing feathers?"

They filed out one by one, goodbyes casual but warm. Tammy paused at the door, adjusting Lockie in her arms. "See you tomorrow." The cat meowed as if confirming his attendance too.

The door clicked shut behind them, silence settling over the back room.

Olivia refilled her mug and let the apple-clove steam spiral upward into her face.

She stepped over to the murder board and traced her fingers across its bare surface. Blank now, but not for long.

Mike's face appeared unbidden in her mind, uninvited. Was he outside somewhere, breath fogging the air while he repaired another window? Flashing that easy grin at someone else? The image refused to dissolve despite her mental shooing.

She gulped her cider and stared out the window. White flakes swirled against a darkening sky.

Thanksgiving approached.

And after that?

Christmas.

And whatever the snow decided to bring.

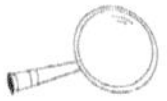

Thank you for reading *Podcasts, Pretenders & Pumpkins!*

Can't get enough of Willowcroft?

Order/Buy

Turkey, Telescopes & Tallmadges

— a Thanksgiving mini-mystery from the link/QR code below.

https://mybook.to/TurkeyTelescopesTallma

(Hint: price increases after launch.)

Book Description

Feast, family, and felonies—just another Thanksgiving in Willow-croft.

With Wally away visiting family in Boston and Xander buried in school-work, the sleuthing squad is short-staffed this holiday season. When Tammy takes a tumble on Willowcroft's icy streets, she expects nothing more than bruised pride and bed rest. But with the team down to just the girls, she finds herself recuperating in Mrs. Temperance's guest room, with a front-row seat to the town's quirks... and possibly its secrets.

Armed with crutches, a telescope, and her ever-watchful cat Lockie, Tammy launches her "Snoop Log," a harmless way to pass the time. At least, it seems harmless until strange behavior starts to look suspicious.

Meanwhile, Olivia is deep in a genealogical puzzle that hits close to home and brings unexpected visitors. But when history stirs up modern danger, uncovering the past becomes more than academic. It becomes urgent.

Can the remaining team uncover the truth in time for the holiday feast, or will this Thanksgiving be remembered for all the wrong reasons?

Curl up with a cup of tea and return to Willowcroft, where mystery is always on the menu—even if you were just hoping for pie.

For even more from Willowcroft and the team, sign up for the newsletter and receive the welcome gift of a collection of deleted scenes from *Podcasts, Pretenders & Pumpkins.*

Sign Up Here:

As a subscriber, you gain access to the password protected "Freebies" page, where all past freebies are kept, including prequel novellas, puzzles and more.

And because you read *Podcasts, Pretenders & Pumpkins,*
you gain access to a webpage that can only be found through this link:

https://franheapwriter.com/ppp-bonus-page/

Here you will find more bonus material designed specifically for those who
have read the book.

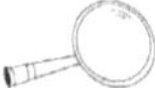

Are you loving the Willowcroft Cozy Mystery Series?
Why don't you leave a review to help other readers find it!

Write your review here!

The End!

The Willowcroft Series

About the Author

Fran, currently living in Melbourne, Australia, has wanted to be a writer since she was nine. It only took her forty years to get there! With two travel books written to test the waters she is now writing cozy mysteries and having a fabulous time doing so. She has no intention of stopping with multiple series planned and begun.

Before her writing life she travelled the world while working as a nanny and neonatal nurse. She has visited 61 countries but aims to visit over 190.

By her own admission, she's a terrible redhead with a penchant for quirky data collecting and thinking outside the box. Her favourite motto is "Curiosity killed the cat, *but information brought her back.*" There is a lot of Fran in Olivia, but also in Tammy too. She loves ancient ruins and drains, hates dusting, loves going behind the scenes, can't smile in photos and detests selfie sticks. In her younger days, she wanted to be an actress, an astronaut, a hostel owner, a department store owner, a doctor and a writer.

When she was ten, she wrote in her diary: *Tonight I vowed I will get a story published at some stage before I die.* She has fulfilled that vow!

www.ingramcontent.com/pod-product-compliance
Lightning Source LLC
Chambersburg PA
CBHW060554190726
48283CB00003B/1005